MAR -- 2017

Fic KETCHUM
Ketchum, Jack,
The secret life of souls /

P9-DWE-914

WITHDRAWN

THE
SECRET LIFE
OF SOULS

THE
SECRET
LIFE
OF SOULS

Jack Ketchum
and Lucky McKee

PEGASUS BOOKS
NEW YORK LONDON

Alameda Free Library
1550 Oak Street
Alameda, CA 94501

THE SECRET LIFE OF SOULS

Pegasus Books Ltd.
148 W 37th Street, 13th Floor
New York, NY 10018

Copyright © 2016 Dallas Mayr and Edward Lucky McKee

First Pegasus Books edition November 2016

Interior design by Maria Fernandez

All rights reserved. No part of this book may be reproduced in whole or in part without written permission from the publisher, except by reviewers who may quote brief excerpts in connection with a review in a newspaper, magazine, or electronic publication; nor may any part of this book be reproduced, stored in a retrieval system, or transmitted in any form or by any means electronic, mechanical, photocopying, recording, or other, without written permission from the publisher.

Library of Congress Cataloging-in-Publication Data is available.

ISBN: 978-1-68177-234-9

10 9 8 7 6 5 4 3 2 1

Printed in the United States of America
Distributed by W. W. Norton & Company

"One does not meet oneself until one catches the reflection from an eye other than human."

—Loren Eiseley

THE
SECRET LIFE
OF SOULS

PROLOGUE

*I*t's six in the morning.

   Delia is deep asleep, sprawled on her side. She's dreamless. For the moment, content. A breeze from the open window drifts a lock of hair across her forehead. She takes no notice.

   Caity lies curled beside her, Delia's arm resting lightly across her belly. But like all dogs, her senses remain alert even as she sleeps. Her ears twitch. She blinks awake. Hears a faint tapping from downstairs in the study. But it's familiar enough. She returns to sleep.

   Delia's twin brother Robbie sleeps too in his own room, dreams of a sailing ship on which he is somehow both captain and cabin boy and then, as is the way of dreams, adrift alone in a capsule in deep space. He is comfortable there, not frightened, his mind at ease.

   His father Bart inhabits a world between sleep and wakefulness, between night and morning. His eyes have opened six times now only to close again. He has glimpsed the rumpled empty space on his wife's side of the bed, the canopy above him, his water glass and ashtray on the end table. He has also glimpsed, in dreams, Jack Dannski and Shiela Lake laughing over bar nuts and whiskey at his high school reunion and his brand-new '62 Corvette tooling through the bright summer wind along the Parkway. These last two moments elude him. He grasps at them with eager fingers.

Delia's mom—Pat, Patricia—is wide awake in her study, poring over photos of her daughter on the computer. Her fingers tap the keys back and forth from photo to photo. Headshots. All of them good because she's hired a very good photographer. But she's quite attuned to nuance, Pat is. She'll easily pick out the best of them. She knows her young daughter's face as well as she knows her own—reflected as it is now in the monitor, ghostly, as though Pat herself were inside the monitor, drifting, overlain, peering out through her daughter's eyes.

Does she detect a wrinkle?

Not a one.

It will be another hour and a half for them to meet in their modern, well-appointed kitchen over coffee and English muffins and begin their morning as a group, as a family.

In the meantime, Caity lies awash in the scent of them, near and far.

PART ONE

PART ONE

ONE

I want you to have a look."

Patricia spears a black olive from her small Greek salad and rolls it in the viscous oil and crumbled feta on her plate.

Across from her Bart holds a baby back rib poised between thumb, forefinger, and ring finger as he studies the owner's manual for their brand-new cherry-red Firebird. Delia munches her charcoal-broiled chicken wing. Robbie pops a mozzarella stick into his mouth and sucks noisily at the spicy red sauce.

Nice thing about takeout from Chicken Little. You can order anything from corn on the cob to a veggie burger, from Philly cheesesteak to orzo to chocolate pudding. The menu's all over the place.

Ribs are the family favorite, though. To this, on the floor between Bart and Delia, Caity bears silent witness. The platter in front of them holds the sad remains of a triple order. Just two left.

Pat slides her iPad across the table to Bart. The image is the one she's selected that morning.

Yesterday was a damn good day in the studio. The photographer, Scott, is only in his late twenties but he has a good eye and can take direction.

And Delia had been marvelous.

They'd sat her on an apple crate in front of a plain muslin backdrop, Caity at her feet. Caity was always at her feet or somewhere within Delia's sightlines whether she was in the shot or not. The dog's a kind of talisman. Pat doesn't mind. Whatever gets the job done.

She'd helped him select the lenses and gels and they got down to business right away. Delia sat up straight, her attitude poised and centered, instantly ingratiating herself to the camera's eye as though they were old friends, she and the Nikon, as though the camera were a living thing, Scott merely a finger on the trigger, Delia giving him just the slightest of head adjustments, a tilt of the chin here, a tiny slide into or out of a hot spot there, exactly what he needed, Scott knowing it was good, the triggerman smiling back at her.

Pat orchestrating the whole thing.

"Okay. Game face on, Delia. Scott? Can you line up on my axis?"

"Sure thing, Pat."

"Okay, march in."

She watched the monitor as he moved the camera closer.

"Right there," she said. "Stop."

And that was where they got the shot.

The soft light imparts a hint of the painterly—but acrylic paint, not oil. Edges super crisp, tones sharp.

Bart bites into his rib, puts down his owner's manual and squints at the shot. She envies him the goddamn ribs. But they aren't a good idea for her. All that fat. All that sugar.

"Nice," he says. "Very nice. But I still don't see why we don't use Mills Photos. We can afford them. Everybody else does."

"Exactly why we shouldn't," she says. "We want hers to stand out. You see the way he's cropped it here? Slightly off-center? Mills Photos wouldn't think of that. But it pops the lighting on her hair. See?"

"Yeah."

"Besides, Delia knows Scott by now. She's comfortable. And it shows, doesn't it."

"True. It does."

Comfortable isn't exactly the right word, she thinks. *Natural* is more like it. Her daughter has the uncanny ability to take an entirely *un*natural environment and shape it into her own living room, her own bedroom, her own swimming pool or backyard. And to do it almost instantly.

They've talked about it. This small skilled leap of the imagination.

"I just see it," Delia tells her. "I see it and it just stays there in my head. For as long as I want it to be."

Pat feels it had little do to with any rapport with Scott. Scott is just easygoing, familiar, and modestly talented. Plus the price is right.

Delia reaches across the table.

"Lemme see."

She smiles and turns the iPad toward her daughter. Once again she's aware of being very proud of her. Proud of her talent, her poise, her enthusiasm.

"I look like *you*!" Delia says.

Pat laughs. "No you don't. You look like *you* in a grown-up skirt and blouse."

Delia studies it some.

"It's okay. I like it. But where's the ones with Caity?"

All her shoots had to end with a few of her and Caity.

"The producers want you, Deal. Not your dog."

"Producers won't protect me from the ghosts, will they. Caity does. She deserves some good pictures."

"Ghosts?"

"Yeah. Like the ones in my dollhouse."

"You mean *my* dollhouse. You're just borrowing it, remember?"

It had been Pat's since she was eleven years old.

"You can have it back. It's weird now."

"What do you mean, it's weird?"

"You know. *Weird.*"

"What are you talking about? You've had it since you were a baby."

"I told you. It's got ghosts in it."

Robbie snorts, grins. Pat interprets. *Little sisters.* Even though he'd beaten her out of the womb by all of seven minutes.

"Nothing in it but a bunch of old furniture, Deal," he says. "You got to relax. You want that last rib?"

Somehow one of the remaining two ribs has simply disappeared. Pat looks down at the floor. Caity gives her one of those *"what, me?"* looks that attempts to deny the three inches of gnawed pork bone between her paws and shoots a glance at Delia. Her conspirator.

Delia ignores her.

"No, go ahead, you can have it."

"Thanks, sis." He reaches for the rib. "Okay if I go work on my models?"

"Sure," says Bart.

"What's wrong with the coleslaw?" Pat asks.

"I had enough, mom. Can I?"

Typical of Robbie, she thinks, to ask approval from both of them. Not just Bart or Pat but both. Robbie's a pretty good kid.

"Wait!" says Delia. "I want to show you guys something."

She gets up and walks into the living room. Robbie chews his rib. Caity does the same, openly and noisily now that the jig is up. Bart goes back to his manual.

She returns with two rubber racquetballs in hand. One purple, one blue. Sits down and turns to Caity.

"According to the Internet," she says, "dogs have trouble telling the difference between purple and blue because they see a more limited speckrum than . . ."

"*Spectrum,*" corrects Pat.

"A more limited spectrum than people. But not Caity. Caity's not color-blind. Watch."

Delia holds both the balls out to her, one in each hand. The dog gets up and sniffs them.

"You can have the purple, Caity. *Purple*."

Without hesitation the dog selects the purple ball between her teeth and sits. Robbie sighs. *Boring*. He may or may not be bored for real. No way of knowing. He's at that age.

"No wait," Delia says. "I want the purple. You can have the blue."

Caity gets up, deposits the purple ball in Delia's hand and takes the blue. Sits again.

Robbie sighs again.

"This is pretty dumb."

"Be nice, son," Bart says. "That's it?"

She smiles and shakes her head and retrieves the ball from Caity. It's showing signs of drool.

She puts her hands behind her back and switches the balls back and forth a few times and then holds them out to her. Palms down this time, concealing them.

"Caity? Dad wants the purple ball. Robbie wants the blue."

The dog sniffs them and nuzzles Delia's right hand. Delia turns it over. *The purple*. She takes the ball in her mouth and drops it in Bart's lap. Then takes the blue ball from Delia's left hand and does the same for Robbie.

"Pretty good," says Bart. "Maybe we should get her a TV gig. What do you think?"

"Not done yet," Delia says.

She gets up and walks around Caity and cups her hands over the dog's eyes.

"*Hide* 'em," she says.

"Huh?" says Robbie.

"Hide 'em."

He gets it. In the spirit of the thing this time. He tucks the ball into his armpit. Bart sits on his.

"Caity, I want the blue ball. Can you get me the blue ball, please?"

She takes away her hands and Caity goes directly to Robbie and immediately starts nuzzling his armpit. It tickles.

"Hey!" he laughs and the ball drops free. Caity picks it up and brings it to Delia.

"Thank you, Caity."

Now where the hell have they learned that one? Pat wonders. When had they practiced? Her daughter's full of surprises.

"Neat trick, Deal," she says. "Now if you'll excuse me I've got to send this photo off to Roman and the printers for their overnight so we can have it first thing tomorrow."

"Can you e-mail me the ones with me and Caity?" says Delia.

"Sure, hon."

Truth be told, some of the shots with Caity are damn good too. She's a Red Queensland Heeler and photogenic as hell. Two-and-a-half years old. Sixty pounds of healthy dog-muscle. A fine delicate ginger color, frosted throughout with white. Dark intelligent eyes with that distinctive black patch over one of them that gives her the look of some kid playing pirate around Halloween time.

Maybe Delia should teach her a few more tricks, she thinks. Get a real repertoire going.

What the hell, you never knew.

His father pushes away from the table.

"I'm heading out to the lift. Robbie? Want to come?"

The Firebird is his father's new toy. What was the word? *Enthusiasm.* That's what his mom calls it. His new enthusiasm. His father is *enthusiastic.* He hoped it lasts awhile. It isn't the kind of thing his dad would consider Robbie really ought to be interested in, where he'd have to be involved, like football or baseball were, or very briefly, soccer. Robbie can get away without not caring too much about the Firebird.

Though it surprises him a little actually. Robbie's good with his hands. His father knows that. So it sort of surprises him a bit that his dad doesn't insist his son join him doing guy stuff out there, tinkering with the chassis or whatever.

"Pass, dad. I'm gonna go mess with the models."

And maybe some other things.

"Right, sure. The models."

"Want some ice cream?" Delia asks.

"Nah," he says. "Maybe later."

He watches them head into the kitchen. First his sister to the refrigerator and then his father to pour himself a drink from the bar.

Caity begins to follow them. He calls her.

"Cait? Caiters?"

She stops and turns.

The pair of racquetballs lie on the table in front of him. He picks them up palms-down and conceals them just as his sister had done and offers them to Caity.

"You can have the purple one," he says.

She cocks her head and takes a few steps forward. Sniffs at his hand. The left one. He opens it.

Blue.

Well, she's Delia's dog, he thinks.

Much as he loves her he has to recognize that fact on a daily basis. Caity is Delia's, not his. She tails his sister like a pilot fish.

With Caity it had been love at first sight, though, for both him and Delia. Ever since that Christmas morning two years ago when his mom had made them wait at the foot of the stairs, all the other presents unwrapped by then and stacked beneath the Christmas tree, while she opened the door to their bedroom and this tiny ball of fur had come bounding out, seeing them down there below and running, skittering on the floor and catching herself just as she was about to go over the landing, pausing, looking bewildered there for a moment before thumping down on all fours onto the first stair and then the second, and finally getting the idea that the stairs belonged to her completely, and flying down them as though with a lifetime of practice.

She'd gone first to Delia and then to Robbie. He'd never seen his sister smile like that before or since.

He can still feel the warmth of her tongue. Recall the smell of puppy-breath. Remember the small tight bulk of her beneath his hands.

This awesome new creature among them.

A dog was magic.

And it didn't wholly matter that she belonged to Delia first and to him only second. He's read up on dogs. He knows about pecking order and pack. Robbie's pack. By rights mom or dad ought to be top dog—*alpha* they call it—*dominant*. They were biggest, loudest. They gave *orders*.

But that doesn't seem to matter much to Caity. Caity has her own mind about things. And in this she turns the tables on the common wisdom. The voice she listens to second most often, second most attentively, is his own, not his parents'. And Robbie is pretty content and maybe even a little grateful that, to her way of thinking, his place in the pack is secure.

He hears the freezer door slam shut. *Ice cream.*

Caity turns away from him and trots to the fridge.

No way he can compete with that.

Stegosaurus, she thinks.

Two scoops of peppermint ice cream—green flecked with choco-late. Three big wavy yellow potato chips stuck on top with a handful on the side for dipping. The potato chips stuck in there give the dinosaur his fins. Though if she were to be really accurate about it what she has here was more like Dimetrodon in fin-size to body-size, which wasn't a dinosaur at all but some early mammal. But she'd been building ice cream *Stegosauri* since she as a little kid and only recently learned that. So whatever.

She crunches into a peppermint-flavored chip and looks down at Caity sitting politely beside her licking her chops.

"You can have one. *One.* Then I'm putting them away."

Caity gobbles up the chip and gazes longingly at the bag on the counter.

"Okay. Two."

She gives her another and rolls the bag closed and seals it with the clothespin against the humidity. Digs into her ice cream.

The dog hops up on two feet and snags the bag off the counter. Then sits down beneath the table, peering out at her from between the rungs of the kitchen chairs, tail thumping on the floor.

"Bad girl! Gimme those back . . ."

The dog gets up and saunters over to the counter. Stands up on her hind legs again and deposits the bag amid the crackers and cookies and other chips that line the back wall between the designer mason jars of flour and sugar. Sits down and wags her tongue.

Delia blinks at her, amused and a little amazed. You just never could tell what this dog was going to do.

"Whoa," she says. "Good one, Caits!"

She plucks a chip off her bowl and feeds it to her. Caity crunches away.

"Come on, you."

She picks up her bowl and walks back through the dining room and into the hall to the stairs.

Caity's eager.

"No running on the stairs, wiggle-butt," she says.

Her dog has a tendency to slip on her front feet, paws skittering against the high polish. She gets to the top way ahead of Delia anyway and turns, waiting on high ground.

"Where's Robbie?" she says. "Where's your brother?"

Caity trots down the hallway to the closed door next to Delia's and sits.

Delia taps at the door.

"Yeah? Hang on a minute."

She hears him close his closet door. His chair pulled out and then back in along the wooden floor.

"Okay. Come on in."

She opens it, sees her brother at his bench table under a single bright desk lamp, the rest of the room so dark so that you can barely make out the clutter of horror movie and Marvel Comics action figures, airplanes, rockets, cars, and trucks that line the shelves behind him. Never mind the posters of Clone Wars, Minecraft, and Elvis on the walls.

The current project is some old car. He's gluing something to the grille.

"Want a chip?" she says.

He doesn't look up. "No thanks."

"What's that one?"

"Flying saucer."

She laughs.

"Nineteen-fifties Buick Roadmaster convertible. Christmas present from dad a few years back. Been sitting here. It's not one of the best model companies in the world—real basic stuff—but I thought I'd give it a shot."

"Looks good."

He shrugs.

She's aware as she so often is that this is his room, his space. She wouldn't dream of sitting down on his bed uninvited, for instance, or browsing through his stuff. Her brother is a private person. Even Caity seems to understand that. Like now. She hasn't budged from the doorway. And while their mom feels free to barge into Delia's room unannounced anytime day or night and do whatever she wants in there, she seems content to let the dust bunnies collect in Robbie's room.

Delia doesn't know if she envies him for that or not.

She does envy him some things, though.

"Wish I could come to school with you tomorrow," she says.

"Right. You wanna trade?"

"I would, if mom would let me."

"You're not missing anything, believe me."

She thinks about Mrs. Strawn, her math and science teacher.

"Gotta be better than some old tutor with salami breath," she said. He laughs. "I guess."

To be honest Mrs. Strawn is the worst of them. No sense of humor. No fun. She likes Mr. Jacobsen, her English teacher. But then she likes English. So she isn't sure how much of that is the subject and how much is him. And she can tolerate voice, though she still thinks Mr. Thatcher is pushing her for the high notes, straining her. He did it again just today running through "I Will Always Love You." She's starting to hate that song.

Her mom didn't agree about his pushing her.

"You're training a set of muscles," she said. "They need the workout. Remember, *I know.* I did this too, way back when. You'll see."

And she has to admit she loves dance. That kind of workout she can get behind all the way. Absolutely. Whether it's classical or modern or even the occasional dip into folk, she loves that feeling of freedom you get after the first half hour or so, that feeling of heat spreading all through your body. And that sense of *rightness* when the moves all work and came together. Dance is great. Dance is fine.

So she guesses that if you balance it all out she isn't doing all that bad.

Still, Robbie gets to see a bunch of kids every day. Kids their age. While all she sees are adults. All of whom are focused *on her,* who want something *from her.* It's tiring. She's tired now.

She's aware that she's just standing there. Doing nothing. With not much to say. Robbie's dabbing some tiny plastic thingy with glue out of a tube.

I must look like a total yo-yo, she thinks.

Time to put it to bed. She'll read a little first. She's well into the third book in the *North Star* series.

"'Night, Robbie," she says.

"'Night, sis."

She steps outside and quietly closes the door.

Okay, now where's Caity?

She'd been sitting right behind her here.

Sometimes that dog is a mouse.

She walks down the hall to her room. Flicks on the light.

No Caity.

Her eyes go to the dollhouse. Her mother's dollhouse. It's modeled after some old mansion in Rhode Island, her mom said. Two floors, four bedrooms, two bathrooms. It's pretty big. Two feet tall, two feet wide and two feet long. And on its built-in wooden table, pretty heavy. They'd had to struggle to get it through the door.

It's been years since she's played with the thing. And she'd never really loved it. She'd always found it a little *too much* somehow. Her mom had made it clear that the furniture and interior were to be handled very carefully. Hand-tooled wooden chairs and beds and sofas. A fireplace of real brick. Tapestries. Paintings on the wall made from a single strand of paintbrush. A kitchen entirely imported from England.

Gramma Atherton had spared no expense on her favorite daughter.

It was pretty to look at. But it kind of sucked when the imaginary kids in the house had to be careful playing with their tea sets and teddy bears.

Where's the fun in that?

So now it just sits, gathering dust beside her bed. She barely gives it a thought anymore. The dollhouse is just there.

Except the night before last.

Except that the night before last, out of nowhere . . .

She must have been nodding off, half dreaming. But she could swear she saw flickering light coming from the top floor, in the bedroom she used to think of as her own way back when she was little, when in her imagination she still inhabited the place sometimes, when she still liked puttering around up there, rearranging the furniture and stuff.

White light. Pop pop pop. An irregular stuttering. Like some big firefly was trapped inside.

It didn't last. Maybe two minutes, tops.

But it was weird.

THE SECRET LIFE OF SOULS

She almost got out of bed to peer inside and get a closer look, to investigate. But truth be told, she was kind of scared.

She wasn't used to being scared. In fact she couldn't remember a single time when she'd *ever* been scared. Not for auditions, not for Mindbender or Wildcat at Frontier City. Not even for Robbie's DVD of *Killer Klowns from Outer Space* for god's sake. Not for anything.

So that chill running down her back had surprised her.

She reached down for Caity at her feet, woke her snorting from her sleep and snuggled along the length of her and they watched together. But there was nothing after that. Before too long she became aware of Caity's easy, regular breathing, the rise and fall of her strong warm chest beneath her hand and pretty soon she was asleep.

Then last night? Nothing. And she'd sort of tried to stay awake just in case. But yesterday had been the tutors and back-to-back acting and dance classes and by evening she was exhausted. She hit the pillow and was gone.

Maybe I should take it apart and have a look, she thinks. Check it out. Three of the sides were removable. One opened to the front hall, stairs, front parlor, and dining room, one to the kitchen, and one to the back parlor, with bedrooms above each. The light had come from the second floor, right over the back parlor.

She considers it.

A funny thought comes to mind. *The house looks at rest now.*

She decides not to disturb it.

Instead she spoons up the last of her ice cream, puts down the bowl, and turns to go look for Caity and uh-oh, maybe she turned too fast because all of a sudden she feels this tingling, dizzy sensation and she almost loses her footing, she staggers. For a second everything goes black. Then the black is shot with streaks of color and light as though she were in a car racing through the night on some wet city street and all you can see is this weird blur.

Abruptly the racing stops. She sees a hand reach out as through a heavy mist toward something bright and shiny right in front of her, not her own hand, though it could be, it's that close to her. But she has the spoon in one hand and the ice cream dish in the other so that's impossible and then the bright shiny thing is a door of some kind only too small to be a door yet it opens like one and inside are small bottles of something or other and then, just as quickly as door, bottles and light have appeared, they disappear altogether.

No tingling. No dizziness. No mist.

Just her room. Her everyday, normal room.

For the second time in two nights she's scared. Not *way* scared but scared. Scared enough.

First the dollhouse and now this.

She needs to find Caity. She doesn't know why but she does.

She walks out into the hall to her parents' bedroom, the only place upstairs she hasn't been in yet, and when she gets to their door, there she is. She can see Caity sitting in front of the open door to their big brightly lit bathroom, sparing a quick glance over her shoulder at her as she approaches.

There you are, she starts to say but just then Caity sneezes. A great big Caity-size sneeze. She does that sometimes.

"Dammit, Caity!" her mom says.

Her mom is standing in front of the mirrored medicine cabinet over the sink. The sneeze has startled her. An empty plastic water glass drains into the sink's scalloped bowl. There are pills scattered all across the marble counter. She gathers them up, but too quickly, knocks two of them to the floor.

"Shit," she says.

She's not aware of Delia yet. Delia's out of her sightlines.

Caity is watching her intently.

"Headache, mom?"

She startles, recovers.

"I guess. Probably at the computer too long. You need to use our bathroom for something?"

She opens the medicine cabinet door. The mirror flashes. She turns the pill bottle in her hand and there's something weird about the way she does that, as though she doesn't want Delia reading the label—which at this distance she couldn't anyway—and sets it down inside. She closes the door.

"I was just looking for Caity," Delia says.

"Well, here she is. And she shouldn't be. Neither should you. Half hour, I want you in bed, young lady. Big day tomorrow. And I told you, no ice cream at nighttime."

"I didn't . . ."

She swipes a thumb across Delia's cheek. It comes away green. *Busted.*

Her mom smiles. So no biggie.

"You e-mail me Caity's pictures yet?"

"I'll do it now. Twenty-nine minutes, kiddo. I'm checking on you two. Better be tucked in."

"We will."

She moves aside and as her mom brushes passed her she gets a familiar whiff of what she knows to be scotch whiskey, mom's drink of choice. She and Caity follow her into the bedroom and then through, out into the hall, and she turns and sees mom seated at her vanity table, combing out her long beautiful hair.

Bart's garage—and it's *his* garage, make no mistake about that—is easily big enough to house three cars comfortably. But what with the new four-poster lift out there and his bar and workshop there's only room for one. He likes it that way. Years ago when the kids were little Pat had angled for a playroom but he'd put the kibosh on that one, saying that she wanted to be able to keep an eye on the kids, didn't she? Especially Delia. And you couldn't do that readily if they were out here messing around with god knows what. She'd folded pretty quickly at the logic there.

As a mother with the kids growing up, Pat was protective if she was anything. Now, less so. But by the time she loosened up a bit he'd long since laid claim and the deed was done.

He pours himself another Boodles gin into a tumbler of ice and takes a sip, studying the undercarriage.

The undercarriage is a goddamn thing of beauty. All low-sheen black. Wheel arches, suspension, exhaust system, all of it completely free of rust or fluid seepage. So clean you could practically eat off the thing.

The price tag had daunted him a bit at first. Thirty-two thousand. Another three and a half for the upgrades. But he wanted the upgrades, even the little stuff—the leather heated front seats and heated auto-dim mirrors, the rearview camera, the Bluetooth, the Universal home remote. All of it.

If Patricia has any complaints she hasn't said so. Delia's been pulling good money. And what with this series hanging fire . . .

They were gambling, he knew that. But gambling ran in his blood, didn't it? His father had been an Atlantic City card-counter for three-and-a-half years until he got himself banned from every casino in town. As a teenager growing up Bart loved to hear dad's stories about the perks and the freebies, about the comp tickets to the Beach Boys and the chorus-girl quim, about disguising himself as a rabbi during the 1964 Democratic Convention or a drunken cripple at Resorts International and retiring with a cool five grand nestled in his pocket and a casino flunky pushing him along to his room in his wheelchair.

He even liked the yarns about those mornings his dad had found himself lying face-down in some gutter somewhere, felled by bad luck and free whiskey.

So they were gambling a little. So what? It made life interesting.

What you didn't gamble on was quality. And the Firebird here was definitely quality. The real deal.

He eases himself down into his canvas-backed director's chair, fires up a Winston with the Zippo, and admires her.

Robbie checks out his work.

On the actual vintage 1950s automobile, the "sweapspear" side molding was a chrome-plated strip that ran from just above the Road-master's front wheel, curved down through the body to the top of the rear wheel and then curled in a quarter-circle straight back to the taillight. But on this shitty model they've broken the plastic strip into two parts, one that runs from wheel to wheel and the second that circles the taillight. Okay. Bad enough. But on the right side of the car they'd gotten the measurements off, just enough so that you practically had to break the thing in half in order to fit it around the taillight.

It's practically finished. That big grille in place, wheels in alignment. But that strip. That damn strip.

He's super-glued it down, so there it is. It is what it is and what it's going to be ever after.

And what it is . . . sucks.

He sets the car down and rolls it a few times across his worktable. Then just stares at it a moment, its pale gray body awaiting a paint job.

I don't think so, he thinks. *Not today, not ever.*

He raises a fist, brings it down hard and smashes it all to hell. Watches a whitewall tire roll across the table.

When the tire shudders to a stop he opens the deep drawer beneath his table and uses the palm of his hand to slide all parts of a would-be Buick Roadmaster convertible off the desk and into the bin below—a bin which already contains the various parts of a Viking warship, Lon Chaney's Wolf Man, the White House, a Boeing B-52 Stratofortress bomber, and various other models which over the years have never quite met with his approval.

You're either worth it or you're not, he thinks.

He turns to his computer and boots up Resident Evil 4 and settles in.

Delia plops down on her bed and takes off her sneakers and socks and jeans and the Lady Gaga Local Crew T-shirt and slips her plaid L.L. Bean nightgown over her head. Socks go in the hamper. T-shirt and jeans she drapes over the dollhouse, covering up all the front windows and the paneled front door.

Ghostie-lights, gotcha.

Caity's at the bedroom window.

"You want out, girl?"

The tail starts going.

She slides off the bed to the window just beyond and folds together the three-paneled screen and sets it on the floor. Caity's out like a shot, her nails clicking along the rooftop. Delia hoists herself up and out.

The night is warm and the breeze light. Together they walk the gentle slope until they're beyond the window's sightlines and sit there and she feels that good sense of privacy she's always felt, that the roof belongs to them and them alone, undiscovered. Down below past their gated yard the streets are silent, winding along in wide lazy semicircles past the houses of neighbors she's never met aside from glimpses on lawn or sidewalk from their passing car and probably never would meet.

People keep to themselves here. They know the Gilmores and the Levys on either side and the McBrides across the street and that's that. And the Levys only to wave hello to in the driveway. Nobody else has kids and nobody has a dog. When she and Robbie were little they used to pretend that they were the only two kids in the world, searching the half acre or so of lightly wooded land beyond their house for others. Finding imaginary traces of them. A broken branch. A depression in the tall grass. A candy wrapper they'd tossed themselves months before.

"Watcha got, girl?" Delia says.

Caity's rooting around in the old faded baby blanket they keep up there to sit on. She comes up with a small green stuffed dragon, pushes it out from between the folds of the blanket with her snout. A favorite toy. She snorts. Exactly when the dog has snuck it up there Delia has no idea.

She reaches for it.

Caity lowers her chin, protective, and stares at her balefully. *Right.* She's *soooo* scared.

"You crack me up, wiggle-butt," she says.

She leans back against the faux-wooden siding and gazes up at the stars through a night without a hint of clouds and a waxing crescent moon.

"One of these nights, girl," she says. "You'll see. I mean, go figure, eleven years old and never yet saw a shooting star. That's not right. Not fair. But when I do, you'll be a witness, won't you."

The dog stares up at the sky. The dragon lies between her paws. Delia scratches the scruff of her neck.

"Yes you will," she says.

"You like the pic?"

Patricia waits in front of the keyboard until Instant Message *bloops* her.

"I do," Roman writes. **"Hot."**

"Hot? Gross," she writes. **"She's eleven years old."**

Bloop. **"You know what I mean. She sells the photo. Hot."**

"Of course she does."

She waits. **"Hubby there?"** he writes.

"Out playing with his car. Gotta sleep. Can't. Not tired."

"Magic beans?"

"How long do they take? Not feeling them yet."

"Patience, Prudence."

She doesn't know where he's gotten the Lunesta and doesn't care. One of his buddies in LA she figures. Some client's doctor. They came in an unmarked bottle and there were fifty of them. A good supply. Now if they just work. It's been half an hour already.

"Need my sleep," she writes.

"She ready for producers tomorrow?"

"Yeah. Just have to keep her focused."

"That's how she brings in the bucks."

"We not she. Team here, remember?"

She sips her scotch and types again.

"Gotta put her to bed. 'Night."

Bloop. **"Nobody in this damn bed but me."**

"Sad. Beans better not be a bust. See you on set."
YrAgent is typing but she closes the app on his response.

Robbie's sprung some traps in the shed and taken out a not-zombie with a pitchfork but that's when they get him. He turns off the PC. Gets up and walks over to his bed and topples onto it like a felled tree. He plumps up the pillows and sits staring at the closet door, considering.

The closet is a spacious walk-in, well arranged initially by his mother and then kept that way, neat and relatively clean, by him. His shirts, pants, and jackets hang from a wooden bar dead center. There's shelving on both sides for his shoes, sweaters, jeans, and sweatshirts, with two rows of favorite books he wishes to keep private just for himself, a row of CDs, another of DVDs, some old toys and games shoved way up top and a sprinkling of his earliest models. Easy, kid stuff. Pieces that aren't good enough to show in the bedroom but which he can't quite see his way to dump yet for some reason.

His tools are shelved there too. The ones he doesn't use every day. Three deep plastic boxes full. He knows exactly what's in each of them.

He stares at the closet and thinks about what's in the closet aside from all this and waits for either sleep or what his father calls a second wind to come along, and one or the other will decide him.

Tonight? Maybe yes, maybe no.

He smiles.

Delia replaces the screen in her window and climbs over Caity's sprawled body to get to her own side of the bed. She's barely settled in with her book when the door opens and there's mom, iPad in hand.

She sits down at the foot of the bed.

"I brought you some Caity pics," she says. "Then I'm off to get some rest."

"You could have just sent them."

"I wanted to check in with my daughter. Problem with that?"

"No."

"You all ready for tomorrow?"

"What's to be ready, mom?" She sighs. *"'Chomp chomp, chip chip, stomp your feet, get those treats . . . yaaaay, Chomp Chips!'* It's so lame."

"Just keep thinking *fun* and *tasty*. That's what you want to keep in mind."

"Chomp Chips taste like lima beans."

Mom laughs. "That's why it's called acting, dear. You inherited a gift. All you need to do is use it."

"Yeah, mom. I know."

"You're gonna do great, kiddo. Scoot over. Let's have a look at these. There's one shot in particular. I think it's your Christmas card."

Delia shifts and makes room for her. Caity groans. They've disturbed her.

"Quit complaining," Delia says. "This is all about you."

The beans are kicking in after all. Between the Lunesta and the scotch she's having a hard time navigating. Beneath the track lighting the polished wooden floor gleams unnaturally bright. She turns toward their own room and among the stills of Delia from age two all the way up to the present—commercial and fashion shoots—which line the walls on either side of her daughter's door, her eye is caught by one of them.

Delia was probably all of four years old at the time—Pat thinks this is about right—posed seated, leaning against the stage prop of an old wonderfully gnarled tree, legs pulled up in front of her and arms clasped around them, smiling off somewhere into the distance. The costume is an elf's costume, kelly green, complete with jagged-cut sleeves, pointy shoes, and a peaked cap around which her hair—permed into curls for the occasion—rises merrily.

It's a department-store Christmas ad—*Come Meet Santa's Elves!*—but every time she looks at it what it brings to mind is not that particular shoot but her own childhood and staying up late with her parents one lovely, magical night to watch Mary Martin in *Peter Pan*. And the song skips fleetingly into mind.

I'll never grow up, never grow up, never grow u-up—not me!

Her daughter as Peter Pan.

And something of herself as well.

She steadies herself against the wall and then proceeds down the too-bright corridor.

She awakens to an unfamiliar scent.

She knows this house, her nose knows every inch of this house, the history of this house and the tale it tells her daily. From the floorboards in the downstairs hallway where eleven months ago Bart spilled a glass of wine on his way to dinner to the spot at the base of Robbie's mattress when, as a pup, startled by the sudden flap of wings outside his bedroom window, she peed a few shameful drops of urine.

But this scent is new. It is still in the process of being created, in fact, as Delia—her Person, her First Person—shifts beside her in her sleep.

It's not a pleasant scent. It is not welcome in a room that smells of Delia, of her clothes in the open closet and her laundry on the floor, of seven pairs of shoes, of the night-dew on the breeze through the window, of books and bedclothes and toiletries and a dish of melted ice cream.

It itches the insides of her nose.

It's faint. But acrid, bitter. She is reminded of the old railway ties they once encountered on their walks through town. Of cans stacked high for disposal in the garage.

Metal.

But its source is the dollhouse. Between the bed and the closet.

Wood.

She's nervous now. More so as a breeze ruffles the fur along her neck. It's not coming from the window. It's coming from the dollhouse.

That's wrong. No breeze should come through there.

Delia's shirt, draped crookedly over the top of it, flutters.

Caity stands. Resists the urge to pace. Her person is sleeping. *But the urge to pace is strong.*

Her left front paw rises from the bed and then falls. Apparently, the paw has a will of its own. Then the right paw. Then the left again. And yes, to her chagrin, now she is pacing. And a whimper escapes her too.

Beside her, Delia wakes.

"Whaaa . . . ?"

She looks to Caity. Wipes sleep from her eyes. Then looks to where Caity's looking, her eyes glued to the dollhouse, tail slicing through the moonlight.

The dollhouse shudders. She detects a thin rattle, as of knives in a sink.

Delia's arms wrap tight around her. She smells of ice cream and deep sleep.

The house shudders again and the shirt slips quietly off the roof and whispers to the floor. Delia's embrace tightens across her shoulders.

"Caity . . . ?" she says.

At the very top of the house a window vibrates. And now she knows that Delia can hear it too. A buzzing sound—an insect in a jar. She can smell Delia's fear, sweaty and sharp as old cheese. Her own body trembles with excitement. Delia's hands grip the scruff of her neck. Delia gasps.

Inside the window, a tiny light flashes. Twice, three times. It holds. Bright and shimmering.

And slowly, slowly, dims.

Delia has backed up all the way to the headboard. Caity stands between her and the house. She feels strong and courageous now. This is her duty. To protect her Person. She sits. She waits and watches.

As the night draws slowly down.

Finally, huddled beside her, Delia sleeps. Her breathing speaks of peace. The danger, if there ever was any danger—if this was not just some curious new aspect of the home she has known for so long and so well—has long since passed. Only then does she allow her eyes to close and her body to sink into the warm nest of blanket, sheets, and bed.

Only then will she dismiss mystery. And sleep.

TWO

How anybody can be so peppy in the morning is totally beyond her. She sure can't match her mom for energy. She'd dragged her butt through breakfast, a hot shower, and getting herself dressed, and now here she is sitting in a chair in the dining room while her mother brushes her hair like there was no tomorrow, all bright and sunny and smiling, while she can still barely keep her eyes open. That it isn't even dawn yet doesn't help matters any. The sky is about as gray as she feels.

She'd better shake it. Because here it is, her *big day* according to her mom. A national broadcast commercial shoot and a meeting with the sitcom's producers afterward, who'd be there watching her work the shoot. So she should be feeling some sense of urgency, some nervousness, some pressure. But all she's feeling is the urge to crawl back in bed and curl up next to her smelly mutt.

She's been trying to tell her mom about last night. But mom isn't having any.

"Now you know why I say no ice cream before bed," she says.

"The light was red, mom. It kept . . ."

She sighs. "There are no lights in the dollhouse, Deal. Gramma had it made when I was a baby. It's not wired for that."

"I saw it. Caity saw it."

"Oh, well, if Caity saw it, it must be true."

Robbie's standing in the doorway, wiping sleep from his eyes.

"What's the word for what mom's doing right now, Robbie?"

"Patronizing you?"

"That's it. Patronizing me."

"Let the dog in, Rob," her mom says.

He opens the door to the patio and Caity slides inside.

"So what are you doing up so early," mom says. "Ghosts in your room too?"

He snags a box of cereal off the counter.

"What? No. Hungry."

"C'mon, mom. Honest. This was really weird . . ."

She finishes brushing. "Get Caity her leash, Deal. Let's get to it. Got your sides?"

Delia digs into her back pocket, pulls out the stapled pages and waves them at her. Her dialogue for the TV show. The audition isn't until tomorrow but with the producers at the shoot today, mom wants her ready to fend off any questions about the character or whatever. She already has them mostly memorized.

"I'll grab my purse and we're outta here."

Robbie pours some cereal as she walks briskly away. Delia takes the leash off its hook and clips it to Caity's collar. The dog wiggles her butt. Adventure time.

"Ghosts, huh?" he says.

"In mom's crappy dollhouse. It's alive."

"Alive? Oh yeah?"

"The window. It was . . ."

Her mom reappears, big purse slung over her shoulder.

"Robbie, try and wake your dad before you catch the bus, okay? C'mon, Deal."

"See ya, Robbie," Delia says.

"See ya."

Break a leg, he should have added.

He does wish her well. Today could mean a lot to her.

He stands in the doorway, cereal bowl in hand, watching through the screen as his mom's Suburban pulls out of the driveway and through the open courtyard gate. He watches until the gate closes up again behind them.

Break a leg, sis, he thinks. Go do your thing. You too, mom. I'll just stand here eating my Wheaties and then I'll wake up dad and then I'll get on the damn bus for the damn school and piss away another day on whatever. And that's my day, isn't it.

Break a freakin' leg.

Pat knows them immediately. A man and a woman in sharp tailored business suits wending their way through the cables, reflectors, lights, and huge mounted silk and sheet-metal flags overhead, which litter the immaculately manicured botanical garden. Today's set. They're followed by another man in shirtsleeves. She pegs him as the writer.

Kristy, the production assistant, leads them along, catches her eye at their video village and waves.

They've just finished a take. A botched take. Delia was fine, ably holding the center spot amid the Busby Berkley–type rows of dancing extras wearing giant toothy grinning foam mouths— *Chompers*—lip-synching their way through the ridiculous guide track. One of whom has just missed his mark and damn near taken down an entire line.

It's been a rough morning. The gusting wind is playing hell with the dancers' costumes for one thing and the sun keeps pulling in and out from behind the clouds. They've yet to get a useable take for the master shot. It's an amiable crew, though. Thus far tempers are fine. She hopes it remains that way.

"Caity? Sit. Stay."

She pats the dog's head, loops the leash around the spindle top of the canvas director's chair, stands, and smiles.

"Mrs. Cross? These folks are here to meet you?"

"I know. Thank you, Kristy."

"No problem. But we're about to roll again in five. So if you could . . ."

"We'll keep it down. Thanks."

She turns to her guests as the girl walks away, talking into her headset.

"Hi there. I'm Patricia Cross."

She holds out her hand. The woman takes it first.

"Polly Hendrix. Thanks for inviting us."

"You kidding? Thanks for taking the time. And you must be Sean."

"Sean Morrison. Pleasure to meet you, Mrs. Cross."

"Pat, please."

"Pat." He shakes her hand. His grip is easily the lighter of the two. "And this is Abe. Abe Joplin. Creator of the show."

Abe's shake's just shy of limp.

"Really fine to meet you, Abe. The script is amazing."

"Is it? What draft did you read?"

Sean laughs. "Abe's a bit sore. Story conference this morning. He's feeling a little beat up around the edges."

"More like bludgeoned. Where's the girl?"

Caity gets up, takes one long look at the writer, then steps over and licks his hand. He pulls it away.

"Caity! Stop! Bad dog!"

Her ears flatten.

"Your dog?" he says.

"Delia's. Sorry."

Joplin clearly isn't a dog person. He looks down at the hand as though she's smeared it with dead fish.

29

"I need to wash this," he says.

He turns and walks away.

Bludgeoned, maybe. Definitely anal.

Caity barks once and with her front paws on the chair seat, gets up on her hind legs and shakes her leash up and over, shaking it free of the loop. She hits the ground running and barks again. Then runs off across the set toward Delia and the milling Chompers.

"Dammit, Caity!"

"Do we go after her or what?" Polly says.

"No, no. She won't go far."

"Don't worry about Abe. His reaction. He's . . . emotional, you know?"

"More like a big baby if you ask me," says Sean. "But you gotta love him, damned if he can't write great dialogue."

"He's very interested, though. Delia's cattle call is the only tape he didn't fast-forward through," Polly says.

"That's . . . well, glad to hear it," says Pat.

We're in, she thinks. *I can taste it.*

Standing to their left the assistant director has his hand in the air.

"Okay! Quiet people! Picture's up!"

Production assistants parrot him into their headsets. Then, but for the gusting wind, the set falls silent.

"Roll sound!" he says.

Sometimes you just know, she thinks. That was the magic of the thing, or part of it. Sometimes you could feel it going just right. And terminally silly as this spot absolutely, positively is, this is one of those times.

The choreography's cheerleader-simple. Her dance teacher would have a good laugh. But there are twenty dancers in the troupe besides her and they were having a heck of a time seeing through their clumsy Chompers costumes—she's glad *she* isn't wearing one—and getting their maneuvers right. This time though, from her initial perfect high-step kickoff straight on through, they were hitting their rhythm, hitting their marks, and you could feel it sweep through the whole bunch of them. *This is going to be a take.*

And then the end, just as she raises her head for that final salute so that her face will read better for the camera and falls ever-so-gracefully into the arms of a pair of the Chompers, a gust of wind goes whistling wildly through the banners and the big twelve-by-twelve silks and sheet metal mounted above them, to terrific effect she can tell, blowing through her hair—which doesn't hurt any either—and then on the final chord of the track, dies abruptly. It's one of those things you couldn't have planned in a billion years but which she knows will add really neat energy to the entire shot.

". . . and *cut!*" yells Curt, their AD. You can tell by his voice he's excited. "Okay, our first usable take, people! Great job, everybody. Great job, Delia. Wasn't Delia great?"

Applause from cast and crew. Cheers. It's embarrassing. She does her best to smile.

"That's lunch," Curt says. "Chompers, please check in with wardrobe before you get pasta sauce all over your costumes."

She walks over toward her mom, standing with some people she doesn't know over at the video village. They meet her on set halfway.

"Hi," she says, breathless. She looks around. "Where's Caity?"

"Probably begging chicken strips off the grips again," says her mom. "Delia? This is Polly and Sean. They're producing . . ."

"*Lip-Lock!*" she says. "I love the title. Makes me laugh every time."

"Glad you like it," says Polly. "You were very good just now, Delia. Very good indeed." Beside her Sean nods assent.

"Thanks," she says.

A man ambles up to join them. Tall, thin, balding.

"Deal, this is Abe," her mom says. "Writer and creator of the show."

They shake hands.

"The script said 'Abraham,'" she says.

"That's right. Actually, I prefer it."

"Abraham, then. Abraham it is."

"I watched you," he says. "You were good."

"So what did you think of the script, Delia?" says Sean. "We're still finessing it, so any suggestions are fair game, right Abe?"

The tiny daggers Abraham shoots at his producer are not at all lost on Delia.

"I wouldn't change a thing," she says.

"Really?" says Polly.

"Well, there was one part I didn't get."

"Only one part?" says Sean.

"Maybe it's just me, but doesn't it seem kind of wrong that Margaret would wear a bikini to the pool party? She seems too shy for that. That felt a little off to me."

Sean's face drops. Abraham's brightens. There's something going on between these two, she thinks. *Hollywood.*

"That's a very good point," says Abraham. "Maybe that was a misstep, huh, Sean?"

She glances away for a moment and sees Caity trotting toward them through the set, which is now abandoned by all in favor of the food trays, her leash trailing.

The wind picks up again and Caity stops, looks up, and sniffs the air.

"I'm looking forward to the screen test tomorrow," Abraham says. "We all are. Delia's tape is great. But I'd like to see how she interacts with Veronica Smalls."

"That's firm now?" her mom says. "Smalls is the lead?"

"Signed the papers yesterday," Polly says.

Her mom actually claps her hands. *Mortifying.*

"Wow!" she says. "Delia? You get to act with Veronica Smalls tomorrow!"

She's seen Veronica Smalls in a couple of movies they'd rented from Netflix when her mom had heard that the woman was up for the part. Light comedies, both of them, in which she played a kind of endearingly scattered mom. That, evidently, was her thing, left over from her days on that old sitcom *Apple Tree Road.* And the script for *Lip-Lock* is basically more of the same.

She's good. That's clear. Delia just hopes she's nice too. She knows that some of the stars aren't.

Caity's by her side now, tail wagging, nuzzling her hand. She gathers up the leash and pets her muzzle.

The producer guy Sean is saying something about how they're testing other kids for the part tomorrow as well and her mom is saying something like of course, that was the business, they're just delighted to be considered, and Abraham is saying something else she doesn't catch, and it's strange and maybe it's the wind blowing hard now across the set rattling the silks and sheet metal above but their voices are all of a sudden fading in and out like some glitch in a movie soundtrack and she feels a little sick to her stomach and a little woozy. Weird.

She looks down at Caity and instinctively tightens her grip on the leash. Black spots dance in front of her eyes. Black turns to yellow. Then to bright red. *Red for stop. Red for danger,* she thinks. This is silly. The shot's over. Pressure's off. So what's the problem? She feels like she's about to pass out like she did that time in dance class when she'd forgotten to eat, like she's about to fall.

Caity is looking up at her. No, Caity is looking up and *beyond* her. And then it's as though she too were looking up beyond her, as though *she too* sees the slab of sheet metal above them shudder and whip side to side, pull hard against its support beams, safety cable, and lighting grid, and *"back up!"* she yells. *"Now!"* and spreads her arms wide, slapping her mom in the chest and everyone stepping back fast, as flag and beams tumble down to the walkway like a huge knife in front of them screeching to the ground.

"Jesus!" Abraham says.

"Fuck!" says Sean. "Fuck fuck *fuck!*"

Her vision snaps back into focus. And she doesn't know how or why this should be but she finds herself still looking not above, nor at the quivering twisted metal at her feet but down at Caity standing below and beside her. It's as though she's seen nothing of this near disaster, as though her eyes have never left her dog at all. And maybe they haven't.

There's a long, heavy silence.

"*Bad rigging,*" Delia says. Everybody stares at her.

It's not funny. Not by a long shot.

But then it is.

They crack up laughing.

THREE

Framed in the rearview mirror, both her daughter and her daughter's dog are dead asleep in the back seat of the Suburban. Maybe that's how they dealt with damn near getting crushed to death. She'd deal with it by getting even.

The first thing she'd done after accepting nervous worried apologies from the director, the AD, and all and sundry was to get on the phone to Roman and tell him what had happened. He assured her that he'd handle it no more gently than the situation merited which meant that he was pissed too, and now, a mere half hour later, he was reporting back.

And now that the full *meaning* of the accident has finally settled in, she can't get rid of the anger in her voice and doesn't try. She runs the whole thing by him again.

"Relax," he tells her. "Those damn grips are officially done in this town and everyone's okay, that's the important part. Trust me, everybody who's needed to have their ass handed to them, has. They've already offered to double her fee. I won't answer their calls and it's only going to drive up the price that much further. Gonna give them the rest of the day to think about it. I'm betting we can triple it, maybe more. I've got 'em shitting bullets right now."

"Excellent."

"We'll put her through college on this one, Patsy darlin'."

Patsy. She ignores it.

"God," she says, "I'm finally starting to come down. I felt like a tuning fork back there."

"Librium working, is it?"

"I'm not Hunter Thompson, Roman. I don't have a pill for every occasion. Just deep breaths."

"You sure they got enough coverage before you bailed?"

"Yes. She had it nailed before lunch."

"Good. And we're still set for tomorrow, right?"

"Hell yes. And I don't know how you see it but I'd say that saving everybody's lives today gives her a firm leg up on the competition. Plus they like her, I could tell, and she was prepped like a pro."

"Which she is. You're a good mom, Pat. Deal's a lucky kid. But I meant are *we* still on for tomorrow."

"Sorry. Mama's got too much on her plate at the moment I'm afraid."

He sighs. "Okay. I hear you. First things first."

She hangs up and pulls into the photo studio's lot. Next appointment of the day.

"Wakey, wakey, sleepyhead," she says. "Time to get us back to work."

The shoot is for Animal Rescue, Delia perched on a bare wooden stool against a white drop, a one-eyed cat named George sitting purring in her lap. The cat's a trouper. Caity, whining on the leash in her mother's hand, is not. Whether she wants in on the shoot or to get at the cat is a matter of conjecture.

But Delia has to smile at her evident distress.

When it's over the photographer, who's been all business up to then, offers her a wicker basket filled with giant jawbreakers by way of thanks.

"Can I take one for Robbie?" she asks her mom.

"Sure," her mom says.

Robbie likes the red-hots, the cinnamon. She digs around until she finds one.

"What about you?" asks the photographer.

"I'm all candied out," she says.

Her mom laughs. "When do you ever hear *that* from a kid?" she says. "I'm a terrible mother!"

After that they get in the car again and there's biology with Miss White, a break for a late lunch at two and then math, and after that a cattle call for some energy drink commercial in which Delia sits alone reading her novel, the third book in the series, awaiting her turn amid a dozen or so other kids holding their headshots and fidgeting, while her mom takes Caity for a walk.

They call her in to the audition room and as they slate her name and age she has a quick flash of Caity staring at a squirrel crawling upside down along a tree trunk and then she's reading from the sides, doing her little-girl thing.

By the time they get home the sun's almost down and Delia's pooped. Her dad has the garage door open and he's standing next to the hoisted Firebird with a drink in one hand and what turns out to be an automobile air filter in the other.

"Did the gardeners take *all* our hoses?" he asks. "Can't find one. How long have we had no garden hoses?"

"Got me," her mom says. "There should be one around. But we don't own any garden hoses. The gardeners rent us theirs. So why buy our own? Waste of money."

"Hey, drop in the bucket," he says.

"Big bucket."

Inside they kick off their shoes. Caity sniffs them as usual and then as usual, quickly loses interest.

Robbie and her dad have already eaten. Her mom lifts a paper towel off the top of a bowl of half-devoured mac and cheese.

"I'll make us a salad," she says.

"Ham in mine, okay?"

Her mom goes to the fridge and starts pulling stuff out of the crisper. Caity scratches at the sliding glass door. She wants out again. Delia follows.

Robbie's at the pool, running a net along the surface, fishing out pine needles and dead leaves.

"Hey, brother."

"Hey, Deal."

"Watcha doin'?"

"Shooting some hoops."

She sits down at the edge of the pool, slips off her shoes and lets her feet dangle in the water. Watches his net skim the surface in broad long strokes.

"How was the shoot?"

"Fine. Kinda dumb. You read the sides."

"Yeah. Jeez."

He shakes some leaves out on the lawn. Caity runs over for a sniff.

"You work pretty hard, don't you."

"Not really. Mostly it's just waiting around. It gets boring."

"Why do you do it, then?"

She shrugs. "It's fun, I guess. Mostly."

"Fun for mom, for sure, right?"

"I guess. So what'd you guys do today?"

It's his turn to shrug. "School. Homework. Mac and cheese. Dad was on the computer a lot."

Caity sits down next to her, snorts, and rests her head on her front paws. Her eyes track the light shimmering across the water.

"Ever wonder why mom and dad don't have *real* jobs?"

"What do you mean? Of course they do. I couldn't do all this stuff all by myself."

"They aren't the ones spending the whole day in front of a camera."

She laughs. "Mom always wanted to, I think."

"You *think*? *Really*? But she didn't, did she."

"She could. She still could. She's real pretty. The guys on the set act so totally stupid around her. They smile and laugh a lot and then check out her butt when she turns around. I catch 'em looking."

"Gross."

He empties the net again.

"Why're you cleaning the pool?" she says. "We pay a guy."

"I like to. And *you* pay a guy. You make the money. Mom and dad just spend it. It's called exploitation, little sister. You ever think about that? What about you? Isn't there anything *you* want?"

The conversation is making her uncomfortable. This isn't like Robbie at all. His being so serious all of a sudden. What the hell's up with him, anyway? What's the problem?

"Anything I want?" she says. "How about a rain hat for Caity. With holes for her ears. A big floppy yellow one."

"What's she need a rain hat for?" he says, smiling.

He dips the net and flicks it, showers her poor dog with pool water. Caity snorts and gets to her feet, indignant, shakes herself off, and lies right back down again. Delia laughs.

"Meanie!"

"Not me. Never. She's my girl. Aren't you, babe?"

Caity looks at him and whines, not unhappily.

"See?"

"I got you a present."

She digs out the jawbreaker and hands it to him.

"Hey! Red-hot. My fave!"

"Yup. I know."

He unwraps it and pops it into his mouth. She hears him scrape it with his teeth. *Chalk on a blackboard.*

"You're supposed to suck it," she says. "Not crunch it. Jeez."

"I crunch. You suck. Good either way."

"Delia? Salad!" Her mom's calling from the kitchen.

They hear the sudden splash behind them and see Caity spring to all fours, alert all of a sudden.

The lizard's a big one—a couple pounds at least—half-swimming and half-clawing at the far side of the pool, trying to get out.

"*Whoa!*" Robbie says.

"Caity, no!" says Delia. But it's way too little too late.

She belly flops into the pool and starts swimming. Robbie's hands fumble at the pole.

"Don't let her eat it!"

He gets a good grip on the pole and dips the net, thrusts it forward at the lizard. It doesn't reach. Maybe three feet short. And Caity is already halfway across and paddling for all she's worth. He dashes around the corner of the pool and thrusts again. And they don't have time to wonder what Caity would have done if she'd gotten there first because her brother has timed it just right, the net comes up from under and scoops a very scared wet reptile up onto the deck.

It lands on its back, disoriented, clawing at the air, head thrashing side to side. Caity's turned and is swimming toward the stairs at the shallow end of the pool as Delia reaches the thing, picks it up just behind its front legs and holds it high, dripping all down her arm as Caity leaps from the water, sneezing and then shaking, splattering Delia and Robbie both with chlorinated pool water, dancing at their feet in excitement.

Delia holds it away from her and rubs its belly with her index finger. Just like that documentary on the Discovery Channel. Which works, which actually does calm it down. The legs stops scrabbling. "*Easy,*" she says, "*easy,*" and both dog and lizard seem to obey. Caity sits back on her haunches. Robbie brushes the water off his shirt.

"Grab her, quick," Delia says.

Robbie kneels and takes Caity by the scruff of her sopping-wet neck. Delia crosses the deck and sets the lizard in the grass well beyond the edge of concrete. The grass, she notices, needs cutting.

"All right, little guy," she says. "Off you go."

The lizard just freezes there and they can see it trembling for a moment and then she guesses it decides that the surprises were over for the time being and makes a run for it, fast. They watch it scramble away in that weird side-to-side alligator kind of gait they have and disappear into the shrubs beyond the lawn.

"Do you think she really would have eaten it?" Robbie says, laughing.

"She would have played with it if we let her, for sure," Delia says. "In the end, same thing probably. Dead lizard."

"Delia Ann Cross! Dinner!" Her mom's shouting now.

Okay, she thinks. *I hear ya. You don't have to scream at me.*

Sometimes her mom's no fun at all.

She turns to go and Caity chooses exactly that moment to shake herself again, vigorously, spraying water all over them.

You're getting the hair dryer, she thinks. Caity can't stand the hair dryer. *Too bad. I reek of wet dog.*

She has almost finished with her mac and cheese when her dad appears from outside at the front door.

"Delivery!" he says and holds the door open for some tall skinny guy in a FedEx uniform wheeling in two giant boxes on a dolly.

"We're going to 4K tonight!" her dad says. They watch him sign a receipt and dig into his pocket for a twenty which he hands the man as he's going out the door.

Her mom walks over and reads the labels on the boxes.

"What is this, Bart?" she says. She's just this short of annoyed, Delia can tell. "We just bought two TVs four months ago."

"You want to watch those muddy old things, I'll send these right back."

She sighs. "I thought we were as high def as high def gets."

"This is higher def. Like twice as good, maybe more. Got one for here, one for our room. The kids can have the old ones. I got a killer deal on these. No kidding. A *great* deal. Robbie? Want to give me a hand with this one?"

"Sure, dad."

Robbie turns to her and when he speaks to her he speaks so softly that only she can hear and there's something in his tone of voice that confuses her. And which she doesn't like.

"Nice of you," he says, "to buy dad a brand-new TV set, Deal. Sweet."

Then he goes to his father and together they haul the box upstairs.

FOUR

I'm sorry, Caiters. Honest."

Her dog looks up at her from the floor beside the bed. Her expression mournful.

She's scorched her. Caity hates the hair dryer in the best of times, hates the rushing heat, but Delia had been daydreaming and held it a little too long a little too close to the thick fur between her neck and shoulder and she'd let out a yip.

Delia pats the bed beside her.

"C'mon, girl."

She guesses she's forgiven. Caity jumps up and nestles in, curled along her thigh.

Which is good. Her mom's tucked her in, promising it was going to be another early morning—*six-thirty for god's sake*—and she needed her sleep. She doesn't have to be at the studio till eleven but her mom wants her to be off-book and the book is five pages. Delia pointed out that nobody else was ever off-book but mom was right, this wasn't some cattle call, this was a screen test, and she should probably know this stuff backward and forward.

So she'll get her butt up out of bed like mom wants and study first thing.

That's her job.

She thinks for a passing moment about what Robbie had said about her mom and dad and their work and her own. But it is what it is, she figures. Really, no problem.

She bends over and kisses Caity goodnight on the top of the head and then plumps up the pillow. She glances at the dollhouse.

"Maybe we did just dream it, huh," she says.

In minutes she's asleep.

"Do our kids really need fifty-five-inch flat-screens in their rooms?" Pat says.

She dry-swallows an Ambien and opens the jar of cold cream.

"Why not?" says Bart.

He's checking the HDMI cables along the side of the set.

"So how big is this one?"

"Seventy. Hell, it's like looking through a plate-glass window!"

He's excited. Of course he is. A great big kid with yet another new toy.

"Wait'll I get the player hooked up."

"You bought a player too?"

"Sure. Don't worry. It was half off."

"Half off of what?"

He smiles that sweet disarming smile of his, which had gone a good ways toward hooking her and reeling her ass in some fifteen years ago.

"Who cares?" he says.

She gets up and ties her nightie together and slips into bed.

"No one, evidently. I'm crashing. Keep it down, okay?"

"Okay, babe. Night-night."

She pulls the sleep mask over her eyes. She can hear crickets through the open window. She can hear him moving quietly around the TV set, the silken rustle of his pajamas. She hears the dim regular beating of her heart beckon her down.

She sleeps on her back, belly up, paws in the air.

She's vulnerable. Knows of no reason on earth not to be.

She smells it first, something to which she is not accustomed. Briefly she considers an approaching storm. But there is no storm.

The scent is carried on a slight breeze that ruffles the fur along the top of her head. It's not coming through the window. The open window is in the wrong direction. This is coming from above her, the headboard. She rises off the bed. Points. Eyes jittering. As a burst of air blasts across her muzzle . . .

. . . and Delia's face too. The girl's eyes fly open. Delia's eyes fix for a moment on the mosaic of silk and sparkles in the canopy above her head and then go to Caity. Caity points. Delia turns on her belly to see where this strange breeze is coming from, up on her elbows as a sudden howl fills the room, a screech, though strangely muted, as though from somewhere far away yet right there in the room, confusing her. It is borne on this same sharp-scented breeze.

She quivers in full protect mode beside Delia who has thrown herself back almost off the bed. She steps over her, between girl and headboard and a rumble begins low in her throat. The room falls still.

She feels the girl's arms around her and smells her fear stronger even than the night before. She leans forward, nose twitching. Old wood, glue, polish, and this newer smell.

Her memory searches to place it.

Burning. But not the fireplace. Not the stove. Not the oven. Not the hair dryer.

And then another grating, screeching scream. Louder. Here and far away. Another impossible blast of air. She yelps. Delia lets out a yell, rolls away off the bed. Caity rises up on her hind legs and paws hard at the headboard, her voice a full-throated, angry bark. Delia rushes from the room. Caity places all her weight into the front of her body, leans forward, pawing, scratching.

Whatever this is that has frightened them she will find it, she will destroy it utterly . . .

"Mom! Daddy!"

He throws off the covers and swings himself up half-sitting as his daughter slams screaming into him, her hands going to his shoulders, clutching at his thin pajamas. Bart flails for balance, head swimming, those four or five gin and tonics not through with him yet by a long shot, no sir, his right hand catching the side of the night table and sending his empty tumbler crashing to the floor.

"What the . . . ? What's going on? Somebody in here? Somebody in the *house*?"

He hears Caity's sharp staccato bark, incessant, insistent. *Scary.* Where the hell was the alarm? The alarm is supposed to be foolproof. He pushes Delia off onto the bed beside his wife—his wife groggy from her Ambien, her scotch, and only barely awake, eyes barely beginning to focus—and swings his legs around.

Delia's on him again, clinging to his shoulders.

"Dad! It's after Caity!"

"What is?"

"The *ghost!*" She reaches over to shake her mother. "Mom! Momma, wake up! *Mom!*"

Her mother murmurs *"whaaa?"* and falls back into her pillow.

Patricia's going to be useless.

If anything Caity's bark is even louder now. He feels a rush of what he guesses is adrenaline and pushes himself off the bed.

Ghost? What the fuck?

Is there actually somebody in his house or is this just some kid's damn fool imagination?

He feels a sharp stab of pain. A shard of glass. His foot. The tumbler.

"Son of a bitch!"

It's a big one, maybe an inch across. *Shit.* It drops off his bloody foot to the floor.

There's a heavy glass ashtray on the table. He picks it up just in case. A weapon. He stands and limps across the room, dripping blood. Not a bad cut, and first things first. Caity is flipping the fuck out in there.

In the hallway he collides with his son.

"Jesus! You scared hell out of me, Robbie!"

"Sorry," he says. "What's going on? Caity sounds like . . . like she's going nuts!"

His son looks seriously troubled.

"Tell me about it."

Behind them Delia's calling to her dog. *Cait! Caity!* He hears tears in her voice. Bart lurches across the hall. And then he's in her doorway. He has no idea what he expects to see in there. But it isn't the family dog trying to tear the shit out of the headboard to Delia's bed. The dog's growling, furious, barking up a storm.

"Caity!" he says. "Caity, stop it! Down, girl! Down!"

It's like he isn't even there.

"Caits!" That's Robbie. Still nothing.

He turns to his daughter. Her face is streaked with tears. "She'll listen to you, hon," he says. "Tell her to stop. Make her stop, Deal. You can do it."

To be honest the dog is beginning to scare him.

"Caity," she says. "Please, girl . . ."

Delia approaches, hands held out in front of her as though she's got some treats for the dog but the dog just ignores her, keeps on digging as though she'd like to go right through the goddamn headboard and then the wall behind it, scoring long pale scratch marks deep into the wood.

". . . stop, Caits . . . down, girl . . . down . . ."

She keeps repeating. *Down. Down. Down.* Until finally she gets a look. Then a pause. Then a longer pause.

At last she settles back on her haunches, panting, staring first at all of them bunched together, looking as though she were stunned by what's just happened to her, and then to Delia only, whimpering, sad-eyed. Delia goes to her and hugs her tight.

"It's okay, girl," she says.

Bart's standing in his own sticky blood. There's a trail of it smeared and spotted behind him all down the hall. He wants to ask *what the hell, Delia?* As though his daughter would have some notion as to what's in the mind of her pet. Which is ridiculous.

"Ghosts," she says.

FIVE

hat second Ambien at two in the morning had been a mistake. Having set the phone alarm for 6:30 had been another. Between the two she doesn't so much roll out of bed as melt off the damn thing. Her head feels stuffed with crepe paper. Her mouth feels and tastes like an old dry boot. She tries to work up some saliva. No go.

For some reason Delia lies curled into the crooked arm of Bart's sprawl, his head hidden beneath a pillow. Caity lies fetal along her daughter's thigh, lightly snoring.

She remembers some disturbance during the night.

But . . . what the fuck?

Bart's feet are sticking out from under the covers. The sole of his left foot has been bandaged with gauze pads stained with dried blood and plastered down with half a dozen Band-Aids.

Sloppy job, Bart, she thinks.

And then once again thinks, *huh? What the fuck?*

She bends down for a closer look. Lifts an edge of gauze pad. From what she can make out the crusted cut has slopped bleeding. So at least the sheets are spared bloodstains.

She nearly wakes him to ask what the hell has happened here but then figures that can wait. Bladder trumps curiosity.

There are blood-spots on the floorboards all around the bed leading to the bathroom and onto the tiled floor. He hasn't bothered to clean up. She sighs.

Bart's always been kind of a slob.

No, she thinks, that's not exactly right. Not a slob. Bart just doesn't *see things*. Things that jump right out at most people. Or certainly jump out at her. Muddy shoes tracking the floor after a heavy rain. The toilet paper roll in need of replacing. Bits of food in the sink after stacking the dishes in the dishwasher. Splattered oil or butter on the burners after he's done with one of his famous chef routines.

She supposes she should be grateful that Bart bothers cooking at all—most husbands didn't—but those last two really bother her. She really gets tired of cleaning up after his cleanup.

He's pretty good in the kitchen though, she has to admit. Has a nice way with northern Italian white sauces and Italian food in general. That comes as a result of his stint as *sous-chef* at Lombardia, where they'd met *lo those many fucking years ago*, Pat waitressing her way through a BA in college—her major in languages for god's sake, with some vague notion of teaching afterward, though her minor, of course, was in drama—and Bart working his way up from busboy to waiter to chef to general manager. Ambitious, he was, after a fashion, in those days.

He'd kept that manager job until two years after they married and his inheritance came through. And they'd had the house. His dad, who'd been highly successful during the housing boom of the '80s and '90s, was one of the original contractors on their gated community and had gotten in on the ground floor. A great deal.

He had so many jobs on so many McMansions that Bart grew up thinking of his dad less as a father than as a weekend foreman who happened to sleep in his mother's bedroom. When head-and-throat cancer from too much booze and way too many cigarettes killed him at age fifty-two, the house was long since paid off and there was a hundred-thousand-dollar insurance policy. So he and his mom were never hurting for money. Then when she died, three days short of his twenty-first birthday—breast cancer this time, she didn't believe in yearly physicals—the house went to him as their only child. That and a hundred-fifty grand. Mom was old-school like his dad. Her own insurance was paid up too.

As a couple they'd dabbled in investing without much success but not too many significant losses either and then Delia had come along. And Delia was cute and photogenic as hell with that bright ready smile right from the beginning. Her first gig was for HuggleBug Diaper Pads at four months old. And they never looked back.

So what is her now—eleven-year-old daughter doing sleeping with her dog in their bed?

She hitches down her pajama bottoms and sits listening to herself pee and puzzles this one over.

Mom obviously isn't buying Delia's haunted bedroom story. He's heard raised voices coming from Delia's room and snatches of conversation but he sure isn't going to get involved, he figures he's got one more up his sleeve before he calls the game and it's another hour before his alarm's set to go off so he just pulls the pillow over his head and goes back to sleep.

When he comes downstairs they're running lines at the kitchen table and barely acknowledge him as he pours himself some cereal and then toasts and butters a piece of raisin bread and sits down to eat. Delia waves to him as his mom herds her out the door to the car and that's that.

He's just finishing up when he hears Caity outside scratching at the sliding double doors. They've banished her to the yard today he figures. No field trip. A measure of how important this audition is to his mom.

No Caity equals no distractions.

"You want in, girl?"

She does. For about five minutes. She snarfs up the leftover kibble in her bowl and slurps down some water and then she wants out again.

Typical.

"See ya later, agitator," he says and slides the doors shut behind her and heads upstairs to get his butt set for school.

Bart has no sooner finished zapping his coffee in the microwave when the phone rings.

"Bartholomew Cross, please."

"Yes?"

"Mr. Cross?"

"Yes."

"Sir, this is Bob over at Krzykowski Audio. You recently purchased a Helix amplifier for your car?"

"Yes. Has it come in?"

"Yes sir, it has. But we're having a problem here. Your check hasn't gone through."

"Really?"

"Yes, sir. Afraid so."

"No problem." *It isn't a problem, is it?* "Let me give you my platinum card."

"Sure, sir. Absolutely."

"Hold on. Just woke up over here . . ."

He crosses into the living room and sees Robbie with his backpack headed out the door.

"Hey, Robbie, wait. Run upstairs and grab my wallet off the nightstand, will you?"

"Bus'll be here any minute, dad."

"You miss it, I'll call you a cab."

"Seriously?"

"Seriously."

His son smiles and shakes his head like, *dad's nuts but in a good way,* and turns for the stairs.

"Take five, Deal," Miss Hinsey says, "I have to take this call."

The dance instructor flips open her cell phone. Delia trudges over to Pat sitting in the hard studio chair and Pat hands her a towel. She sits down beside her and pats her neck dry above the leotard.

"I don't get it, mom. What's this have to do with a pool-party scene for god's sake?"

Delia's being cranky. Has been ever since this morning when she'd told her to *please cut it out with the ghost nonsense, will you?* and that she should have more important things on her mind.

Namely, her audition with Veronica Smalls.

"Body language is everything, Delia," she says. "It's not just about the lines. You need to act with your whole body. Caroline's going to loosen you up. You want to be loose, don't you?"

She grabs her by the upper arms and shakes her side to side. Gets her laughing finally despite herself.

"See? Loose as a goose."

"Mo-om!" But she's smiling.

Miss Hinsey's phone snaps shut. "Okay, Deal, *up,*" the instructor says. "Let's do some more work with the shoulders and neck. *Sooo* much tension there . . ."

Pat sits up straight in the chair and does her own shoulder rolls and works her breathing along with them. Neither one notices. Or if they do, don't care. She does this pretty much all the time. Follows along. Two for the price of one, she thinks. Why not?

Dean Kaltsas and Billy Tambour are shooting hoops when he steps out of the cab. According to his watch the bell has already rung five minutes ago but as usual Dean and Billy are pushing it. He crosses the macadam.

"Whoa!" says Dean. "What? Limo driver call in sick today? You should fire that asshole."

"Eat me," Robbie laughs. He's used to taking shit from these guys. "Pass the fuckin' ball!" he says.

They've got time. Dean does.

Caity stretches out to her full length on the lawn, smells the fresh-cut grass, the trees beyond, bird guano and rabbit droppings. Already at this early hour the earth is warm beneath her belly. She yawns.

The old swings creak on their chains, the sun glints on the tarnished metal slide.

Slide. That's a fine idea.

In a second she's up and running, in another she is barreling up the slide, paws slipping on its sleek surface but momentum and sheer bulk carrying her to the top. At its peak she sits and listens to the breeze flowing by, around and into her delicate ears, a soft susurration, a tingle, the breathing world a simple comfort.

She scans the horizon, always familiar yet always fresh with nuance. The bend of a branch, the shadow of a leaf, blossom, birdsong, the drone of bee and dragonfly, the fall of chestnut, acorn, pine cone, their jump and roll and settle on the ground.

And here, now, the scent of fur still damp with morning.

Her tail wags, twitches.

Something out there.

Bart sits at his computer, transferring money from his brokerage account to his bank account. *Two thousand? Five?* What the hell, he thinks, go for five. Don't need this happening again.

Too bad he's always been lousy at math. *Dyscalculia* they called it, like dyslexia only with numbers. He's been that way since grade school. Reversing numbers. Omitting numbers. And here he is handling the family's finances.

The irony is that Pat's much better at it. But Pat isn't interested. In high school and college she'd been an actress, and that's still where her heart is and what she knows about—and if she wasn't ever a really *terrific* actress, if the rejections had finally gotten to her to the point that she'd want to call her shrink after every audition, it was still her area of expertise and the best way for her to contribute to the family.

So he'll crunch the numbers. And if the numbers crunch him now and then, so be it. He likes the implicit risk involved, the possibility that he might fuck up, he likes beating the odds forever set against him. The same as investing.

Make it ten, he thinks, and clicks *Enter*.

Her mom was right, she guessed. She does feel good and limber from the exercise, which has even lasted through all Joyce's primping and pampering with hair and makeup at Rose Blanche. Though that's one part of the business she isn't the least bit fond of.

"They have makeup people at the studio," she'd said.

They'd already been walking through the salon's parking lot. It was a futile gesture toward a last-minute reprieve.

"You need to look the part when you walk in the door and shake the first hand, kiddo," her mom had said.

So Rose Blanche it was.

And Delia figures she was right again. Because when they arrive at the studio and she's greeted by all those dark suits, Sean and Polly among them, she feels like her own personal beam of bright light has just entered, waiting to light up the scene.

Even Abraham, the writer, is wearing black today, though in his case it's a turtleneck and faded black jeans. He seems really happy to see her and brings her over to meet Veronica Smalls.

Smalls is sitting in a folding chair and actually gets up to warmly shake her hand. She guesses the story about the accident has gotten around. Smalls is . . . well . . . *smaller* than she'd thought, and older-looking, clusters of lines around her eyes and mouth and what she'd bet were implants puffing out her cheekbones.

She'd never get that done to her. Not in a billion years.

But they talk all through makeup—makeup *again*, though just touch-ups for Delia—and she seems very nice. She knows how to talk to kids. In fact she talks to Delia like she's just any old other actress. Which is perfect. Delia's relaxed and she's ready.

She's going to nail this.

There's something in the bushes beyond the strong wire fence. Her nose twitches. Her tail beats a one-two, one-two-three rhythm for just a few seconds, then stops. She braces, calculates, and from her perch atop the slide nimbly vaults the fence. Lands on all fours on the old downed lightning-struck oak tree trunk which smells of rot and burn and mildew. Hops from there to the woodland floor.

A rustling sound. There, *amid the berries.*

She has tasted the berries long ago. They turned her stomach. She trots over.

She's identified the scent now. Rather, she's eliminated what it isn't. Not dog, not rabbit, not cat. Not squirrel or mole or chipmunk. Her scent memory counts down like the hands of a clock, its seconds fast approaching twelve.

Fox. The scent is fox.

She needs to be careful now.

She leans into the bushes, nose sniffing rapidly but head inclined downward slightly and to the side. Nonthreatening. Pokes deep and then relaxes. Her sight has confirmed what her nose has already told her. A small gray head with tiny black eyes appears. A kit. Not an adult. Not some wary mother armed with vicious bite and claw. A kit.

Two of them!

She'll stay alert. Their female will be near.

But meantime . . .

Three noses touch and sniff, pull back away and touch again. The one nearest her, the male, marks her with his scent-gland, sliding his small wet cheek across her own and tentatively paws her muzzle. Then rolls over on his back, exposing his red-and-white-patched belly. His sister pounces immediately. And then she's forgotten momentarily as they tussle.

She butts them with her snout.

They break apart, stare at her as though they've only just seen her there. They blink. Who is this creature? She knows she's impressive. Her head's nearly as big as both of them put together. But they're not dissuaded. They venture out from beneath the bushes, hopping like toads. And next second they're all over her, play-biting at her neck, pawing at the thick fur there, climbing on her shoulders, falling off and climbing back again. She rolls and they sprawl across her belly. The female swipes a teat.

Fun!

Delia's nailed it all right, just as she knew she would. Between today and the commercial yesterday she figures she's having one heck of a good run. At the end of the scene she and Veronica Smalls are supposed to exchange this great big hug. Kind of teary, but kind of smiley too. A kind of *awwwww* moment for the audience. All sitcom as hell.

But when they actually do it, it feels natural, absolutely real, like real life. As though they really were mother and daughter having this sweet moment together. So that when the director smiles and quietly says *cut* Veronica Smalls plants a kiss on her forehead that isn't in the script at all.

The kiss says *thank you.*

The kiss also says, *hey kid, you're in.*

She was going to be in a sitcom. A *network* sitcom. The pilot for one at least. With a real-life movie and TV star. Who likes her work well enough for an affectionate kiss.

The second female lead for god's sake!

She crosses the studio floor and gives her *real* mom a big hug.

Robbie and daddy are going to be proud of her. She wishes for a moment that there were somebody else to tell. A whole school-full of other kids. Then dismisses the thought.

She can't wait to hug Caity. Caity'll do.

The tree stump is a springboard from which she clears the fence without the slightest hesitation once she hears the SUV pull into the driveway.

She's done this many times before, though never with an audience of fox kits watching.

She waits in front of the sliding glass doors. Sees them enter the house, her butt wriggling back and forth against the floor. Her butt can't wait to express her excitement.

Delia comes straight over, slides open the doors, lets her inside. She leans into the girl's embrace.

"You'll never believe the day I had, Caits," Delia says to her.

Caity's tail-language says the same.

After dinner she and Caity sit outside on the roof together. It's a little overcast so there aren't too many stars. She can make out the Big Dipper and Betelgeuse in Orion's right shoulder but Rigel below and to the left is obscured by puffy clouds.

She sighs. "I'm tired, girl," she says.

Caity cocks her head as though trying to puzzle out what she's saying. Delia strokes her shoulder.

"It's a good tired, though, y'know?"

She gazes down into the faux-gaslit streets below. Sees the distinctive super-bright headlights pulling out of a driveway two cul-de-sacs away.

"Mr. K's coming over. See there?"

She points. Caity just looks at her raised hand. She points again. "No. Look."

This time she gets it. They watch the car turn onto the road and wind its way slowly in their direction.

"We better get down. You be nice now, you hear?"

She isn't always. Something about Mr. K.—Roman—seems to get under her skin. She'll sulk or move away. Delia can never figure out why. She thinks he's nice enough.

Maybe it's his cologne or something. Or that Oklahoma drawl.

She stands and sighs again and gazes a final time into the quarter-moon night sky. Caity follows her example.

"We'll see one," she says. "Just you wait."

They make their way back through the window.

She checks herself out in her bedroom mirror. Her hair needs brushing so she does that, then has to pee so she uses the bathroom. Caity waits patiently outside the bathroom door.

The doorbell rings as they bound down the stairs.

Mom's on the couch watching CNN. Robbie sits beside her playing some game on his PSP, tapping away.

"Want to get that, Deal?" mom says.

She opens the door and there's Roman, smiling that thousand-watt smile. He's carrying a small box under his arm, wrapped in brown paper.

"Hey there, pretty girl."

He ruffles her hair. *She's just finished brushing it!*

"Hi, Mr. K."

"I hear you were terrific today."

"I was," she says, laughing.

She steps aside for him to enter and out of the corner of her eye sees Caity back away, ears lowered. She emits a low growl. Almost a purr.

Not quite.

"Caits," she says. "Cut that out. Be good."

"Bad dog!" says mom. She's on her feet, crossing to Roman. Reaching out to touch his arm and kissing him on the cheek, guiding him into the living room.

"I was going to call," he says, "but then I thought, some things you got to do in person."

"Like what?" mom says.

"Like this." He hands her the box. "Hey there, Rob," he says. "How you doin', pardner?"

Robbie smiles and waves and continues tapping. Delia motions to the spot mom's vacated on the couch and Caity hops up to sit beside him. Robbie barely notices her. He's into his game.

"What is it, mom?" she says.

Mom's got the wrapping off and opens the box. Her smile just gets bigger and bigger.

"My god! The deal memo! Roman!"

"Congratulations, Delia Ann Cross," he says. "You're a series regular. Fittings start first thing tomorrow."

"That fast? Oh my god. You really did it, honey."

It's official, then. She's aware that in some way or other, her life has just changed. She wonders exactly how. Mom hugs her tight.

"Cool," she says.

Even to her ears that sounds pretty lame. *Cool.* But what else can you say? Mom doesn't seem to notice though.

"This is amazing! Robbie? Think you can handle living with a TV star?"

"I can manage." He smiles and shrugs and goes back to his game.

"Well, aren't we all just a great big heap of rapture!" mom says.

"Congratulations, sis," he says.

"Where's the head of business affairs?" says Roman.

"With his other woman. The garage."

"I need his John Hancock on this. You want to read it over?"

"Not my department. Go right on out. He'll be delighted. Can I pour you a drink?"

"Sure can."

Roman has never given a whole lot of thought to Bart Cross. Not nearly as much thought as he does to the missus. Bart strikes him as an easygoing kind of fella who maybe drinks a bit too much but not so's you'd worry about him or be offended, who doesn't have much truck with ambition or more ambitious types like Roman himself but who doesn't make big a point of it either, who likes the money well enough though. And who sure does like his toys.

Right here's the latest. A nice new Firebird. Pretty as you please.

Bart has the hood up, dipstick in one hand and rag in the other.

Roman runs his hand over the gleaming front fender. Not a speck of dust.

"You stud enough to ride this here mare, ol' buddy?"

Bart smiles. "To a lather," he says.

Roman waves the papers at him. Bart looks puzzled, sets the dip-stick down on his work table and wipes his hands with the rag. Then it dawns on him.

"You kidding me? She got it?"

"Awaiting your signature, my friend."

"I'll be damned."

Roman points to the transmission.

"You know you're supposed to check that with the engine runnin', right?"

"'Course I do."

But he didn't. Roman can read him easy. He hands him the papers and a pen.

"Hell, yes!" Bart says. "Let's sign these puppies and get ourselves a drink. We need to celebrate! Girls doin' their dance yet?"

"There's a dance?"

Bart laughs. "You'll see." He signs.

Inside the music's blaring. Donna Summer, "Love to Love You, Baby." They'd barely heard it in out the garage. Nice insulation.

"Well ain't that sweet," Roman says.

Pat and Delia are in the middle of the living room floor. Good lord, he thinks. *Disco moves. Four-on-the-floor.* He hasn't seen that since the baby boomers quit booming. Robbie's watching his mom and sister like some wise indulgent old uncle. Caity circles around their feet like a spotter in a gym, looking for somebody to fall and possibly bust their damn fool neck.

Patricia's seen them come in and points to a drink waiting for him on the counter. His scotch. Bart pours one for himself. Pat's glass, he notices, is half empty.

"Who's the star?" Pat shouts above the music.

"You are!" shouts Delia.

"No, *you* are. Who's the star?"

"I am!"

"You are!"

Then together, *"You're the star!"*

Roman clears his throat. "They, uh, do this all the time, do they?" he asks.

"Ritual," Bart laughs. "Every big job, each and every one . . ."

The dog was looking at him.

The damn dog has stopped dancing around the dancers and is looking at him. Then the dog is walking toward him, ears flattened.

He feels a shiver race down his backbone. He doesn't much care for dogs. Not dogs of any size, at least. No reason that he could think of for that. No childhood trauma or anything. He just doesn't. Dogs are *other.*

Bart notices his discomfiture.

"Wow, Roman. She likes you about as much as I do."

"Why thank you so very much, Bartholomew. Would you . . . ?"

"Sure."

He reaches down to her, ruffles the fur behind her ears.

"Hey there, Caits," he says. "Want a treat?"

She knows the word. Instantly she's indifferent to him, focused on Bart, her tail a metronome gone berserk. He steps back from her anyway. Bart snaps his fingers.

"Come on, Caits. Treats!" He calls back over his shoulder. "Hey, Rob, come give me a hand here, will ya? Come throw some snacks together."

The boy drops his PSP onto the couch and follows his dad and the mutt into the kitchen.

Bart watches his son pull a veggie tray out of the fridge. He leans in close. Robbie flinches. Probably he smells the booze. Who cares? He has his son's attention. He winks. *Co-conspirators.*

"Listen," he says. "Mom's doing nothing but celebrating tonight. Got that? We take care of her for once."

Robbie smiles. Robbie's a good kid.

"Sure, dad."

Caity's turning circles on the kitchen floor.

"Where's Deal keep the treats?" he says.

Robbie points to the cabinet over the dishwasher.

"Caity gets to celebrate too, doncha, girl?"

Wooof! she says.

Delia sits back in the overstuffed chair, winded. Her mom plops herself down next to Roman on the couch.

"So, you think it'll have a healthy run?" mom says.

"With Veronica Smalls? They're already getting heat for season two and they haven't shot a frame. The pilot is strictly pro forma."

He brushes aside a stray strand of hair clinging to her face.

"You're frizzing," he says. "You guys always dance when you book a gig?"

"We do."

Roman runs his hand down the length of her hair to her neck. Delia catches the gesture and frowns. Isn't that just a little too . . . *intimate*, maybe . . . for agent and client? She kind of thinks so. It makes her uncomfortable. But hey, she thinks, theatre people. What does she know?

And then, watching them, her vision blurs.

She blinks and sees the very same gesture in instant replay. Only close-up this time. Hand running over her hair. The tips of his fingers. The smooth skin of her mother's neck.

Then Caity is suddenly in the room. Barking, skidding across the floor, landing with a crash on the coffee table directly in front of Roman, magazines flying, ashtray shuddering, Caity perched there and barking at him as he tries to merge with the couch, nowhere to go but stuck there with what must seem to him a great big angry monster practically in his face.

"Caity!" Delia yells, shocked.

Her father appears from the kitchen, a bag of Tempty Bits in his hand.

"What the fuck . . . she just *bolted!*"

"Caity!" Her mom grabs her dog by the collar, and furious, yanks her hard off the table, paws frantically scrabbling for purchase. She yelps once and then just stands there, silent, cowering up at Pat and then runs, tail between her legs. Delia gets up to follow. She's scared. But Pat shoves her right back down into the chair.

"Mom! You hurt her! That was so *mean*!"

"Mean? Did you see what she just did? She's crazy! That's it. She's sleeping in her pen tonight."

"What? No, you can't do that!"

"I can't? You just watch me, young lady."

"It's not fair. She was just being . . . *protective*!"

And why that word should come to her she doesn't know.

Not then.

Pat slams down the dregs of her drink. They don't know it but it's her third.

She's burning.

Goddamn dog, she thinks. The goddamn dog's everywhere. Always underfoot. The dog has to follow them everywhere they go. Needs to be around for everything they do. Shoots, auditions. Delia insists. Delia *always* insists. Sometimes Pat's sorry she'd ever bought the goddamn thing.

Well fuck her. Fuck the both of them.

Protective?

What the hell does that mean? The dog was dangerous was what she was.

And now everybody's looking at her. Looking at her like she's some bad guy. Her husband. Robbie standing behind him. Her daughter. And poor Roman, downing the remains of his own drink.

Everybody.

She turns to her daughter. Who is now seeing fit to give her lip. Jesus!

"I want you to go brush your teeth and get ready for bed," she says.

"At 8:30! Are you kidding?"

"You heard me. Get to it. You have a fitting at . . . what time, Roman?"

"Seven."

"Seven. And you are going to *sleep* tonight, you hear me? No more games. You've got . . . we've all got big responsibilities now. Go. Brush your teeth."

Delia sits there. Simply folds her arms across her chest and stares at her.

Defying her.

Calm, she thinks. *Easy, woman.* She takes a deep breath.

"You boys put the dog in the pen and then have your drinks. Delia and I are going to straighten out a few things. Aren't we, Delia."

"Pat . . . it's no big thing . . . ," says Roman.

"Come on, Delia." She reaches down and none too gently takes her daughter's arm. Lifts her off the chair. Practically has to drag her to the stairs. Delia tries to pull away.

"Ow! I hate you."

"You'll get over it."

In the bathroom upstairs she *guides* her to the sink. Slaps the hairbrush into the palm of her hand.

"Brush," she says.

"Mom, please. Come on. Look, I'm really sorry. Honest. Please don't put Caity in that cage. She hates it in there!"

"She should have considered that before she went all Cujo on our guest."

"Dogs can't consider."

"Yes, but you can. Consider this. Two minutes, then straight to your room. Brush."

Where's the damn dog and what's he, Roman, doing looking for her? His papa had always told him to be a good sport but this was maybe pushing it. She isn't in the kitchen. They've checked under the table, in the open walk-in closet. She isn't in the downstairs bathroom either.

The pantry. The low growl tells him as much.

Between the kitchen and the outside door. A dog-sized crack in the doorway and no light on inside.

He backs off again. Third time today if you count the couch and he definitely counts the couch.

"Uh, Bart? Robbie? She's in here."

"Your drink's on the counter," Bart says. "I'll take care of this."

"You got it, my friend," he says.

Delia stands outside the door to her room. She doesn't want to go in there. Not without Caity. *Bedtime? Ghosts again? Yeah, maybe.* And forget the ghosts, Caity's her sleep-mate. This sucks. She hears her mom's heavy footsteps behind her and turns. There's a tall glass of water in her hand.

"Mom? I can't sleep in there. Not without . . ."

"Yes, you can."

". . . not without Caity. Mom, I'm sorry. Caity's sorry. Couldn't we . . ."

Her mom gives her a little push. Not rough, but purposeful. She walks Delia over to her bed. Moves her hand to Delia's shoulder and eases her down. She holds out her hand.

"Take this. Wash it down."

A pill. Delia *never* takes pills. A baby aspirin maybe sometimes but that's all and rarely even that.

"Why? What is this?"

"Something to help you sleep. Take it."

"No."

"Delia Ann Cross. I have not spanked you since you were four years old."

My god, she thinks. She's serious.

I really think she would. She could try, anyway.

She takes the pill, turns it over in her fingers. Such a tiny thing. It doesn't *look* dangerous. Part of mom's stash.

"Swallow it."

"Mom, I really don't want . . ."

"I don't care what you want, Delia, not right now. Tomorrow is *important*. Maybe the most important day of your life. Do you understand that? Do you? You need to sleep. Here."

She plucks the pill out of Delia's fingers and holds it inches from her lips.

"Open."

I hate this, she thinks. It isn't right. Important or not, I shouldn't have to do this. All of a sudden she feels close to tears. Where's Caity when I need her? she thinks. Dammit! She opens her mouth. Takes the pill offered up to her and drinks. One big gulp of water. *Done.*

Her mom sits down next to her and strokes her shoulder, trying to soothe her.

"I'm sorry, honey," she says, "but we need to keep you on track."

Mom strokes some more. Delia isn't soothed, isn't comforted.

"You should be excited, Deal, for god's sake. Tomorrow? It's a whole new game. We're proud of you, baby."

And she isn't excited, either. Maybe tomorrow she would be. But right now she's something else.

She stares at the dollhouse. Stares hard.

"I want Caity," she says.

SIX

What the hell? thinks Bart. She's growling at *me* now?

She's wedged herself between the vacuum cleaner and the laundry basket, her back to the wall. Ass down and paws planted firmly on the hardwood floor in front of her. Glaring at him. *Daring him.* He tugs gently at her collar.

"Okay, c'mon now," he says. "That's a good girl. C'mon . . ."

He drags her six inches or so, slides her across the floor. She won't get up.

This isn't like her. Not at all. What they had here was basically a pretty damn placid animal.

He tugs some more. She yelps. Though he doubts he's really hurt her. This is all fucked up.

"Caits, it's okay, c'mon, I'm sorry, girl. Get up, will you?"

Finally she does. And that's good because he's beginning to seriously sweat here. He leads her by the collar to the door, where she stops dead in her tracks. Feet planted and ass-to-floor again. He can see the pen outside through the plate-glass doors and obviously so can she. She looks up at him. And now her eyes are sad.

Better sad than mad, he thinks. Much better.

"Oh, come on, you big baby. It's just for the night."

He opens the door and she allows herself to be led to the big wire chain-link cage just beyond the slide and swing set. He hauls her in, shuts the gate and locks it. She whines and scratches at the wire.

"Sorry, girl. Mom's orders. To be honest, I'm not all that nuts about that ol' hillbilly con man either."

Cait barks. He decides to take that to be assent.

She lies in dusty old hay spread across the floor of the cage and the blanket on top of that and these scents are both good and familiar—they speak of her, of her sleep—though the sharp metal scent of the cage itself is unwelcome as always. She watches Bart close the glass door behind him and reach for a bottle on the counter. She knows the smell inside the bottle and it too is good and familiar unless too much of it courses through Bart's body, mingling with the other odors which are specific to him, drowning those scents in the tang of anxiety as they often do, as they have done only just moments ago.

She knows to some degree she has caused this anxiety. She dislikes this cage but she is happy to be free of him out here. Free of her responsibility for him as she is responsible for all of them.

She will lie here then in her own scent and all the night-scents. In the insect chirp and the flutter of bat wings, the one fodder for the other. She has no choice. She submits.

Roman has finished his drink and gone and then it's just the three of them down there and the house seems very quiet.

"So what do you think, Rob?" she says.

He looks up from his game. "Think about what?"

"Your sister. The show."

"It's good, mom. It's all good."

"It is, isn't it." She sips her drink. By now it's largely ice.

"I wasn't too mean to her, was I?"

"To who? To Deal?"

"Yes."

He's looking at her strangely. As though he doesn't quite understand the question. Though it seems to her the question is clear enough.

"Not really. Caity was being a jerk. And Delia just . . ."

"She can be bratty sometimes, huh."

He frowns, then smiles. "I don't know. She's probably just tired."

"Tired. Yes."

She gets up to pour herself another. Just a short one. Reaches over and mussed his hair.

"You're a good brother, Robbie," she says. "We love you."

"Same here, mom." He yawns. "I'm tired too. Goin' up to bed."

Caity sees.

This is nothing new to her. This she has been able to do for as long as she can recall, at the first touch of a little girl's hand along her back, at the first salty taste of her cheek and chin on her tongue, the first scent of her silky hair. With all these senses she now surrounds Delia and sees. As, when she wishes, she has always done.

Delia sleeps. In the tiny window of the house beside her bed a red light sputters to life and holds. Growing bright, brighter. A blast of air ruffles her hair, slides along her face. Caity can feel its unnatural strange caress. She sniffs at her cage, the damp tang of metal. She searches for some weakness there.

In the bedroom, a muffled yipping screeching sound, the same as they'd heard the night before. It grows louder, the flow of air around Delia's face stronger. Why doesn't she wake? The light in the small window in the small toy house beside the bed begins to spark. All these things together and at once her search is urgent. She paws at the cage. Delia sleeps on. Caity hunts for access to her sleep, hunts the cage for egress. The light spits and sparks.

She finds it. A thinness to the wire near the top right corner of the cage. She goes at it with her teeth. She can hear her heartbeat lavish in her chest. She goes at it with her paws. A toenail splits, cracks. She tears with her good strong teeth again. The thick muscles of her neck and shoulders bunch and pull. She rips the corner free. Tastes raw metal. Tastes her blood.

The tiny window bursts.

She can see it, smell it, hear it against the ghostly yawning. Sparks fly. Smoke trickles into the air, shaken and dispersed by the air strangely blasting from the headboard.

And inside the small house, beside the sleeping Delia's cozy canopied bed, a flame blooms.

She tears at the hole she's made, rips downward with her jaws, inserts a paw and rears back. Blood and spittle fly. There is panic now and an aware-ness of time. Time inside the room, time inside the cage. She whimpers, rears and pulls again, hurling both front paws against and through the opening, all her weight and muscle bearing down.

The small house is on fire.

Her head is through the opening. Not enough. Wider. *She backs away and clamps her jaws to the section she's pulled free, yanking, shaking. Wire savages her mouth, froths her cheeks.*

The small house is on fire. A chunk of roof falls to the floor, rolls to a stop directly under the canopied pole at the foot of Delia's bed.

She launches herself into the hole. Head and shoulders plunge through but then she's trapped, half suspended a foot above both the lawn ahead and the floor of the cage behind her. Wire scours her belly. She wriggles, struggles, muscles tight as bowstrings until finally the cage disgorges her back and hips and she is free.

She races to the glass double doors, slams against them again and again, barking, roaring her distress.

"Jesus, *now* what's her problem?" Bart says.

He's just brought a full bottle of Widow Jane Seven-Year Kentucky Bourbon, a bucket of ice and two fresh glasses to Pat at the living room coffee table, where she sits composing announcements for Delia's web-site, Twitter, and Facebook pages. She'd been delighted to see him.

"That dog's had a problem all goddamn night," she says. "Let her bark her damn fool head off for all I care. You pouring?"

"I'm pouring."

He stubs his Winston out in the ungainly ceramic ashtray Robbie'd made for them in the fourth grade.

But what the hell's that thumping sound? he thinks. Where's that coming from? What's going on here?

Light flickers, dances glowing through the bedroom window above her head. Fire. She backs away, turns, dashes across the lawn past the table and chairs where they often share with her their midday meal. Dashes to the tree. It's a pinyon tree. She has tasted its bark and sweet nuts. Its branches reach nearly to their rooftop—Delia's and hers. She hits the tree at a dead run, breath whooshing from her chest, climbs its trunk like a squirrel, makes it halfway up the trunk before her purchase fails and falls four feet down onto her side.

She's aware of pain, in her ribs, her hip, and thigh, throbbing through her body. She's dizzy. Inside the room flames climb the canopy of Delia's bed. Steady, spreading, white to black. She smells scorched walnut, bubbled lacquer, and burning cotton. She gets up, shakes her head, runs back across the lawn, turns, and runs again. Hits the tree just right.

Her left paw finds a branch, then the right. She hauls herself up, runs the limb in perfect balance, and leaps to their roof, the roof they share, to the screened-in window between her and Delia inside, Delia finally, at last awake now and coughing, batting at flaming falling debris overhead. Her eeeeeeeeeeeee sails through the screen. She is under attack.

Caity backs away to the roof's edge as the canopy disengages, comes loose, falls. Instinctively Delia has thrown up her hands to protect her face but that is exactly where it falls, onto hands pressed tight to her face, onto bare arms, neck and head. The screen is thin wire mesh and tears and flies clattering away off its track as Caity's full weight comes crashing through and she lands hard beside Delia on the bed. Flames climb down Delia's twisting, rolling body. She springs over and across her, into the flames, flattening herself against Delia's body beneath and she can smell her own fur burning and Delia's hair and flesh burning, smoke rising between them as she bites down hard on Delia's arm and tears her hand away from her face, she must!—and as she screams and screams, drags her off the bed.

Rob stands in the open doorway. In a single moment he takes it in. The dollhouse aflame, the bedcovers aflame, his sister and his dog rolling burning across the floor. *Ohmygodohmygodohmygod. What have I done?*

Only moments ago he'd been . . . *playing.* Just messing around. He'd been standing in his closet making these spooky, eerie noises and blowing hard into the length of garden hose piped into her room through the adjoining closet and up to her headboard, messing with the electric dimmer switch that popped the lights he'd secreted in the dollhouse, having real good fun scaring her over the past four nights, the scares escalating—orchestrated nicely if he did say so himself, kind of a power thing, sure, and a little cruel, but so B-movie dopey he was surprised she bought it—having great good fun until just now when he pushed the dimmer to the max and all of a sudden it started sparking, sputtering in his hands and he dropped it to the closet floor, kicked it out of the closet away from his clothes and shoes and into the bedroom, then stomped on the goddamn thing until it was dead.

He smelled burnt wiring. Then moments later, another burning. Not electric. Something else. *Her room!*

He tore open his bedroom door and ran out into the hall.

"Mom! Dad! Fire!"

Then he heard the screams.

And he was suddenly in her bedroom. Seeing what he'd set in motion. Frozen by what he's done and what to do next and where to go, *the dog his sister the bed* and thinking stupidly stunningly *water, water!* until his father shoulders in behind him shouting *jesus fucking christ!* and rips off his shirt, diving on top of Caity and Delia and rolling, smothering the remaining flames, and seeing this at last releases him. He rips what's left of the burning canopy down off its posts and stomps it out while his mother screams and tears the sheets off the bed and does the same.

Then it's quiet but for their breathing.

The smell of smoke.

And the burning of things he does not wish to name.

SEVEN

He slips into his father's examining room and quietly closes the door behind him. The nurse gives him a nod, then snips off the bandage on his father's forearm and wraps it gently with beige adhesive hospital tape. The nurse is young and pretty. Probably only ten years older than he is.

"There you go," she says. "Be good as new."

"Where's my wife?" he says. "She with Delia? My daughter?"

He seems a little out of it, sits back heavily against the raised examining table.

The nurse is tapping something into the stand-up computer.

"I believe so, yes. You just relax a little while, Mr. Cross. Stay comfortable. Can I bring you anything? Glass of water? A blanket?"

"No. No thanks."

"I'll come back for you as soon as we have word from the doctor."

Robbie steps aside for her and she goes out the door. It's only then that his father seems to notice him. His father sighs and shakes his head.

"Dammit, Robbie. What the hell happened? I can't believe you would . . . I mean, what the hell were you thinking, son?"

I was thinking about me. About Delia. No. I don't know what I was thinking.

"Are the police . . . ? Are they still out there? I just don't understand, Rob. This is bad, son. This is real bad."

"They're gone. They said that for now they just want us to stay together . . . for Delia. There'll be a . . . a hearing I guess. Later. A judge. God, dad, I'm so . . ."

"Sorry? Well yeah. You damn well should be."

His dad must have seen him flinch because he softens then.

"How's your sister? How's Delia?"

"I don't know. Mom won't talk to me. Won't say anything to me. Nothing. Last I heard they were putting her in some sort of . . . a tub . . . to clean out the wounds."

He's seen the wounds. The wounds are red and black.

"Jesus, Rob. Jesus."

She stands outside the emergency room. She can glimpse hurried activity within. Behind her nurses, doctors, staff, file by. She barely takes notice. Her hands have stopped shaking. She clenches them into fists, allows them to relax. *Clench, relax. Clench, relax.* She concentrates on her breathing. Deep, from her diaphragm. Measured breaths.

You use what you've learned.

The double doors swing open and Dr. Ludlow hurries past her to the nurses' station. *Past her? He doesn't see her standing there? He's ignoring her?*

He's holding up a chart, talking to one of the nurses. The pretty blonde who'd gone off with Bart.

"Dr. Ludlow? Dr. Ludlow, please . . ."

He hands the nurse the chart. She smiles a wholly professional smile and moves away down the hall.

"Hi, Mrs. Cross. The nurse is going to fetch your husband and your son. Won't be but a moment."

"Please . . ." *Tell me it's fine. Tell me it's okay.*

And she is actually *reaching for his sleeve*, she would never do that, never, she can't believe it, not in a million years, when the emergency room doors swing open again and three of them, nurses in scrubs, come through pushing a gurney and handling oxygen and monitors and an IV drip which depends from and is attached to that gurney, and on the gurney is a small figure which she sees to be her daughter, Delia, intubated and unconscious, tucked into clean white sheets, sterile dressings covering her entire face and head, being whisked along efficiently past her.

Her breathing stops. She staggers. The doctor takes her arm.

"Hey. Hey, hold on there."

He moves her to a chair. She backpedals along with him. He sits her down. He sits too. And she can hear it in his voice—the doctor is seriously pissed.

"I told them to give me a few minutes alone with you before moving her over to ICU. Obviously they weren't listening. I'm sorry, Mrs. Cross. Really sorry. Hard to see that, I know."

Why do doctors always say that, *I know?* she thinks. They *don't* know. They don't know what you do. Not what you feel deep down in your blood.

She falls back to what she does know. What is sure and certain.

Her breathing.

He follows the nurse and his father down the hall, blinking against the bright lights and shivering against the cold. Their refrigerator back at home, he thinks, has nothing on the hospital's rooms and hallways.

Meat wouldn't spoil here.

His mom is sitting with the doctor. Mom looks pale. Hands clasped in her lap. Back military-straight. Hard. Cold. Her lips pressed tight together. He can see the bristle-thin lines along the top and sides of her mouth.

The doctor doesn't smile.

"Mr. Cross, Robbie. Have a seat." He leans forward.

"Delia's suffered from smoke inhalation and there are second and third-degree burns over roughly twenty-five percent of her body. Luckily, they're mostly second-degree. She's on high-flow oxygen to keep her breathing passages open. Fluids against the possibility of burn shock. And we've got her on antibiotics to prevent infection. It's a blessing that she was quick enough to cover her eyes. They're virtually unharmed. But I've got to be honest with you, her face is another matter. Face, neck, shoulders, arms? They're going to take a good deal of grafting."

His mom seems to sag, almost to relax. Though he knows that is nowhere near true.

His dad clears his throat. "Will she be okay?"

"Yes. Absolutely. We'll have her on an exposure therapy protocol right away. What happens is, the skin's allowed to dry so that the burns form a crust, which peels away after a couple of weeks to expose the healthy skin beneath. We use saline gauzes to soften up the dead skin and speed up the process."

"The burns . . . they'll heal though, right?"

"Yes, they will. But there will be scarring. How much we can't know as yet. But it's going to take time and a lot of tender loving care on your part. She's going to need extensive surgeries. You need to prepare for a pretty long haul here, I'm afraid."

He pauses, looks each of them in the eye. To let that sink in, he guesses.

"She's also suffered a compound radial fracture to her forearm."

"The dog," his father says. "Caity. She pulled her out of . . . pulled her off the bed."

"So I'm told. Well, unfortunately she pulled so hard that she fractured Delia's arm. But the good news there is that it's easily treatable. That dog probably saved your little girl's life, Mr. Cross, Mrs. Cross."

His mother gives Robbie a glance. *You did this*, her glance says. He blinks down the tears and looks away. Something hard coils in his chest. It hurts.

"So we'll keep Delia in ICU for now," the doctor says. "We want her separated for the time being. Infection. But we've arranged it so that you can see her. There are observation windows in that wing."

"See her?" his father says.

"Yes. But only if you think you can handle it. Your wife's already asked to stay as close by as possible."

His dad looks from his mom to Dr. Ludlow and then back again.

"She has? Well, yeah. I think . . . sure. Robbie?"

"*No*," his mother says. "Neither of you."

But Robbie reads, *no, not Robbie. Not him.*

She's gone from sitting there stone cold to fierce in an instant. He wouldn't be surprised if she stood up and hit him right then and there.

Even the doctor seems uncomfortable.

And Rob has no defense for it. None. She'd be perfectly right to hit him. To beat him to the ground. So that now he has to really fight back the tears. Shame and sorrow and fear all rolled up tight together. He turns away.

"You two go home," she says. "Check on the dog. I'll stay with Delia."

"Hon . . . don't you think . . . ?"

"*Go. Home.*"

They have their orders.

In the hallway they're accosted by a smiling, harried-looking woman in suit and glasses. She holds a clipboard pressed to her ample chest. *What did hospitals do before clipboards?* Bart wonders. He's wary immediately.

She introduces herself as Annie Gilbert and they shake hands.

"Mr. Cross, may I see you a minute? About the insurance?"

He tells Robbie to wait for him in the waiting room and follows her.

Her office is bright and uncluttered, the computer front and center on her desk, with nicked wooden bookshelves and dusty filing cabinets off to one side. A tired-looking plant of some sort perches on the windowsill. The pocked white walls bespeak a certain age and lack of care.

It's a business office badly in need of a makeover. As though business doesn't matter all that much here.

Somehow he doubts that.

She gets right to the point.

"I've already called Blue Cross Blue Shield," she says. "Your policy's lapsed, I'm afraid. Two months ago."

"Well, we were . . . we're close to getting an upgraded health benefit status with SAG, so I . . ."

"SAG?"

"The Screen Actors Guild."

"Oh. You're an actor, then?"

"No. My . . . our daughter is."

"I see. I'm sorry, Mr. Cross, and I know this is likely the last thing you want to concern yourself with right now, but . . ."

"No. It's okay. It's okay." *It fucking isn't. Not at all.* "Can you bill me?"

"Certainly. But we're going to need some assurance that all of these procedures can and will be paid for. You understand."

"Of course they'll be paid for."

He pulls out his Platinum card and hands it over. Not without certain a tinge of trepidation.

He needs to be sure of this.

"Where are we now?" he asks. "I mean right now. With the treatments, the expenses? I'd like to pay that much right away. Whatever it takes, you know? For Delia. For my daughter."

She holds up a finger. *Give me a moment.* Turns to the computer and types.

Then turns the screen toward him.

He reads it. Holy shit, he thinks.

Robbie dials the animal hospital and watches his father pull out into traffic. His father looks tired. Almost as bad as his mom did when he left her, her face sagging and exhausted. This is all on him. Of course it is. On his stupid, stupid prank. He'd told his sister a hundred times now that he was sorry. But there was nobody there to hear him.

"We're on our way," he tells the receptionist. "We're . . . how long till we get there, dad?"

"I don't know. Half an hour? Forty minutes?"

"Thirty minutes. How is she? Is she . . . ?"

The woman tells him she's transferring him to a nurse and puts him on hold. He waits. The nurse's bright voice assures him that Caity's sleeping peacefully, that her upper airway had swollen, that they'd had to punch a hole in her trachea. *Trachea was her throat. Caity couldn't breathe.* Jesus. But that the bottom line is, she's all right. She's going to be fine. They can visit.

"Can we take her home?"

"No. I'm afraid not. We're going to want to keep her overnight. For observation. She's had quite a time of it, hasn't she. Quite a night."

She sure as hell has.

He remembers the rich thick smell of burning hair. The wheezing as the emergency driver lifted her into the van to drive her away to the animal hospital. But mostly he recalls her eyes as the guy closed the door on her. The eyes so sad, so confused. As though she couldn't remember what had happened, where she was.

And that was on him too.

He says goodbye and closes the phone. "The nurse said she'll be okay, dad," he says.

"That's good," his dad says. "That's very good."

But it's like his dad isn't really there either.

Robbie is alone.

Roman hands her the paper cup of steaming black coffee and takes a tentative sip of his own. Chock full o'Nuts it isn't.

"I'm tired, Roman. Very tired."

"I know. I know, darlin'."

She damn well looks it. But she's a whole lot more than just tired too. Her reflection in the observation window is ghostly white. Overnight her entire life has changed in ways none of them could have expected. Life could do that to you, he knows, he'd seen it before. Build you up, shoot you down, and spit on your shoes. But what in hell are they going to do now? Pat and her family. Roman's got other clients. He'll get by. Delia isn't the only one paying the bills by a long shot. But this one has been looking big. Damn big. He hates to have to let it go. He's put off calling the producers for that very reason—figured he'd wait until the docs had laid out the entire deck for them, assay the situation.

He's talked to the docs. The situation's grim.

He'll have to call this afternoon.

He puts a hand on her shoulder and squeezes and feels her lean into him, a gentle pressure.

"I can't stand this," she says. "Take me home, will you?"

He extends his arm over her shoulder and pulls her close. Her hair smells of smoke. He doesn't mind.

"Get me the hell out of here."

"Sure I will," he says. "Sure."

She lies in a crate. More bars, new bars. *Her paws are bandaged, and her chin and underbelly. A small tube depends from her throat. It whistles as she breathes. This confuses her. There is no pain, instead a great lethargy that causes her eyes to droop, her mouth to drool. Her tongue sluices the length of her mouth, over and back again.*

In a cage across from her lies an ancient cat, a male tabby with long hind legs and a broad round head and no tail. The cat regards her through a single eye. The other eye is covered with a bandage. The cat smells of old age and medicines similar to her own. The cat yawns. His breath smells of low tide. He closes his eye and sleeps.

Caity closes her eyes too.

Miles away from her Delia is a prisoner of machines. Machines which click, drip, contract, and expand. Her bandaged arm twitches, an involuntary jerk, which Caity can feel in her own right front leg, shooting up from her paw. A needled tube which connects to her arm falls loose. A machine beeps, flashes.

A woman whose lower face is covered by a mask goes directly to the machine. Picks up the fallen tube and reinserts it into Delia's flesh, a pinprick. The beeping stops. Delia sleeps.

Caity lies down on her side and settles in.

She sees fire and smoke coming from Delia's window.

She sees the fire rain down, Delia's hands flung over her eyes, sees inside those hands, the yellow of skin and muscle, the blue-white of bone.

She sees herself vault from the tree, her legs pumping, sees herself burst through the window onto the flaming bed. Smells smoke and burning flesh and hair.

Delia's set broken arm moves inside its pale white shell. Her body goes rigid, fists clench, heart races, the scent of fear pouring off her body.

Caity bites down hard on the arm and hears the splinter of bone inside. No matter. She drags her from the flames.

Sees her own eyes wild.

Then black. A moment of black.

A murmur. "Caity?"

There is the sound of lapping water. A sparkling river. The feel of a light breeze across our back. A fish rises from the water, tail slapping water across our face. Our face is dripping wet. We're on a small fishing boat floating downriver. Behind us Robbie and Bart sit beside a quiet motor, laughing as Bart flips the fish up into the boat, the fish depending from hook and line and wood flapping at our feet. It's a beautiful spring day.

We see a turtle drop off a log, a blue heron cleaning its wings on an old wooden dock, a cave on a bluff, an eagle's nest, a frog jumping from rock to rock. We hear Bart's and Robbie's and our own laughter, smell earth and water and tall river grass. Our body relaxes into the rhythm of the slow drift of water all around us which is the rhythm of our breathing.

We sit and lie in the sun.

Lie forever in the sun.

She types in the security system code on the touch pad. Roman follows her inside. They've said nothing in the car getting here and she is grateful for that.

Inside the phone's ringing. She sets down her purse and checks the caller ID. Her mother. New Hampshire.

She'd made the obligatory call about Delia last night. Her mother was drunk when she picked up the phone and more so by the time the call was over. It's what time now? Five o'clock EST or thereabouts? That means she'll be drunk by now too. She'd been pounding it back hard for going on seven years, ever since her father had hit a patch of black ice on his way home from work at the accounting firm one gray February evening and skidded into a particularly sturdy, particularly lethal low-hanging branch of an elm tree, which took out the windshield, his glasses, and most of the top of her father's head.

The accident had occurred at four P.M. on a Friday. Four P.M. daily was the hour her mother started boozing.

She's not answering. Let it ring. She's got the machine.

"How about I pour you a drink, girl?" Roman says.

"Good god, yes."

The irony of her musings just now doesn't escape her. But she is not her mother.

He disappears into the kitchen.

She stands gazing up at the staircase, listening. *For what?* Something alive and moving. Some echo maybe. The house has never seemed so empty. She feels she doesn't belong here, in this place. That it is not hers to inhabit. Strangers live here now.

"Here you go."

He hands her the drink. Corn whisky. His favorite. Not her own. It doesn't matter.

"Take me to bed, Roman," she says. "They're at the vet's. We've got time."

In the bedroom she fucks him. They do not make love. She climbs on top of him and takes him down with her into sharp broken crystal, bloody shards of glass, shearing knives, and blunt tenpenny nails. She thrusts him through stone.

When it is over she spreads her body over him in damp cooling heat as though to smother him.

"Smoke," he says.

"What?"

"It's gonna be a while I guess before that goes away."

"If ever. I may smell that stink forever."

"Can I open a window?"

She nods. He rises off the bed and pads to the window nearest them and slides it open and the thin sweet-scented breeze of springtime makes her want to scream. The world outside wants in. The world outside is sick with normalcy.

"Finish your drink," she says. "And then I think you need to go. Bart and Robbie'll be back soon."

He sits beside her. His upper body is practically hairless, like a child's. "Whatever you say. Sure. You should rest."

"Rest. Yes."

Who is this man to her now? she wonders. How does he fit into what's left of her life? How does he matter? And when he speaks it's as though he's questioning that too.

"I'm so damn sorry, Pat. So sorry, darlin'. Wish there was something I could do."

"There was. And you did. I needed to . . . to not think for a while, you know?" She reaches over and touches his hand. "Thank you, Roman. Now go, hon. Go. Okay?"

"Okay."

When he is gone she sits naked on the bed for what seems a very long while. Then at some inner alarm gets up and performs a quiet whore's bath in the sink, crotch and armpits soaped and splashed and patted dry, slips into her nightgown and lies back again as moments later the car pulls in and doors slam shut and in the hollow aftermath someone's life resumes, with or without her.

EIGHT

He watches his dad toss the box of burn cream and the pet-cone—a plastic lampshade kind of thing—on the passenger seat of the car as the veterinary assistant wheels her out in the crate. She looks so pathetic in there, bandages on all four paws and chest, wobbling around, all woozy-looking, blinking in the bright morning sun.

He wonders how she'd slept last night. Caity knows the vet's office. They've been coming to Dr. Marder since she was a pup. But upstairs, where they do the boarding, would be all new to her. He wonders if she'd been hearing barking and whining and cat-cries and fear-sounds and sounds of pain all night. Maybe that was why she's still wobbly. Or maybe it's the drugs.

He'd slept badly himself. He'd have bet everybody did. Though mom and dad have their own drugs.

He'd sat awake reading *Rachel Rising* for the umpteenth time, figuring he knew every panel pretty much by heart by now so it would naturally put him asleep. It hadn't. It was too good, Rachel and Jet and Lilith and the rest were just way too off-the-chain a bunch of characters. What he needed was something really dull to knock him out. He needed *Staring at Your Shoes and Other Stories* or something.

And then there was that smell to remind him. Faint, but there. And what he'd heard. And what he'd seen.

Instant replay of the worst game highlights ever.

He'd managed a couple hours after the voices coming from mom and dad's bedroom died away.

The assistant who looks like a college kid maybe, not much older, opens the cage, unbuckles the side fasteners, and lifts off the top half of the crate.

"Sometimes they don't want to come out," he says, smiling. "It's easier just to take it apart. Do you have one of these for her in the car?"

"No," Robbie says. "Can I . . . is it okay if I carry her?"

"If you think you can lift her, absolutely."

"I can lift her."

The guy steps aside for him and Robbie leans down, slides one arm under her front legs and the other under her butt, lifting slightly, judging the weight of her.

"Watch her chest. Lean her on her side."

He does. Takes a breath and holds it and lifts. Not too bad. He can manage. Barely, he has to admit. But manage.

She looks up at him sleepily and he pulls her closer. She shifts, hurting. He adjusts his arm beneath her hips. That's better.

"It's okay, girl. C'mon. We're gonna go home."

His dad has the rear door open. He pushes the front seat forward, giving him room.

"I'm staying with her, dad."

"Sure. Good idea."

His father takes his arm supporting him as he backs up and carefully sits. He turns and gets his legs up and inside and adjusts her on his lap.

"You guys okay in there?"

"We're good, dad."

His dad slams the door shut and he can hear him thank the attendant. He gets in and starts the car.

As they pull out of the driveway he looks down at Caity and at the same moment she looks up at him. Their eyes meet. He can see no blame there.

She's glad to see me, he thinks.

As though to affirm that, she licks his face good and proper.

She's glad I'm here.

He waits for the garage doors to open and carefully pulls in. He turns off the ignition and glances in the rearview mirror and that's when he sees her. Some woman standing outside there, curbside, mid-thirties he guesses, a good-looking blonde and tall, probably taller than him, in print blouse and jeans, smiling.

He gets out and walks around to Robbie's side and opens the door. He doesn't know whether to ignore the woman or what. He's never laid eyes on her before. But he can't very well ignore her because there she is, taking a few tentative steps forward.

"Hi," she says. "Hi there."

Robbie has his arms around their dog but now he notices her too as he shifts Cait's weight off his lap and gently onto the seat and slides out of the car.

"Can you handle her?" he says.

"I can do it, dad."

Robbie leans in to gather up the dog, trying to figure out the best place to put his hands. Bart looks down the drive. She's taken a few steps closer, stands about ten feet in front of the garage.

"Mr. Cross? I'm sorry to bother you."

"Now's not a good time," he says. "Not buying anything."

He's instantly aware of how rude that sounds. And then he thinks, *yeah? So what? Who the hell are you?*

He's in a mood.

"No, you misunderstand. I live up the street in that turquoise monstrosity right there. Number seven." She points.

"Oh?"

He guesses she takes his reply as an invitation. She walks up to the rear of the car.

"I heard about the fire. I wasn't home, but my husband saw the emergency response vehicles and I . . ."

"What can I do for you, Miss . . . ?"

He asks, even though now he gets it. He knows what she wants.

"Leda. Leda Botolf."

"You're a reporter."

She smiles. "Anchor. Channel Three."

"Dad? Can you get the door for me?"

Robbie has her in his arms, her head drooping over his shoulder.

"Sure. Sure, son. Give her my chair in the living room. It's the most comfortable."

He moves to open the door to go inside the house. Then holds it while Robbie steps through, turning to the side to avoid the frame.

"Oh my god," the woman says. "The poor thing. Oh, I really had no idea it was so . . ."

"There's no news here, Mrs. Botolf."

She smiles again. "Jack . . . my producer . . . would definitely disagree with you, Mr. Cross, which is sort of why I'm here. I'm really not asking for a story from you, honest. We're neighbors. And no family should be bothered at a time like this."

"Thank you," he says and thinks, *then why are you bothering me?*

"But I felt I ought to warn you that other stations, the papers, might not . . . see things the same way. Because of the work your daughter did. And I thought that you should probably prepare yourself for . . . well . . ."

"I get it."

"I just wanted to come over and say that if there's anything I can do for you folks, please, by all means, just ask."

She turns to go and then stops herself.

"This is going to sound . . . I don't know . . . strange. But I lost a kitten in a fire once. When I was a little girl. In our basement. And I never quite . . ."

She smiles and waves her hand in front of her face as though to say, *silly me.*

He gives her a long look. Decides he almost trusts her. Almost.

"That's very nice of you, Mrs. Botolf."

"Anything at all," she says.

"Thanks, we appreciate it."

She turns to go.

"Isn't Carrie Donnel the anchor on Channel Three?"

Channel Three was local. He rarely watched it.

"She was indeed. I replaced her last winter. They haven't gotten around to changing the billboards yet."

He laughs. "Once they put 'em up, they seem to stay up forever. There's one of Delia at three years old still up over on Rangeline . . ."

Reality comes crashing in.

What the hell am I going on about? Delia at three years old? Jesus!

She seems to sense his sudden discomfort. She nods, bows her head slightly. "Take care, Mr. Cross. Sorry I troubled you."

"No problem," he says. "No problem."

Her sister calls. She doesn't know why but she takes the call. Her big sister's calls mostly serve to annoy her. But when she sees her number on the cell phone she sets the cardboard coffee cup down on the cafeteria table, notes the pale smear of lipstick along the rim, and for some reason decides to answer.

Hospital reception's surprisingly good. Evvie's voice comes through loud and clear.

How is she? What's going on? How can I help?

I'm so sorry, Patty.

The concern is there. Her sister's good at concern. She's evidently gotten the details of the accident from their mother so at least she's spared all of that. But what is she supposed to do here? Reassure her? What the fuck does she want?

"I can be on a plane in a minute," she says.

"We're fine, honestly. We don't need any help, Ev, really."

"You sure? In a minute, I swear."

More like twelve hours, she thinks. Her sister lives in a small semirural town in northern New Jersey, most of it still farm country. After her divorce, her single suitor was the local postman. Her husband had run off with a supposed friend of hers, a neighbor a mile and a half away.

They're all losers up there. Her sister's no exception.

Alone. All of them. Miles apart. Days go by and her sister won't see a living soul. Evvie says she prefers it that way. She's got the television and she's got her books.

Books. It was always books. Even when she was a kid she always had her nose in some damn novel or other. Evvie was four-and-a-half years her senior so when their mom and dad went out Ev was babysitter and that meant tiptoeing around the house so as not to disturb her reading because it was *too dangerous* to go outside alone until she was at least six or seven or so. Pat had to be quiet. And she hated the goddamn quiet, hated it.

She'd turned the postman down. But he still stops by for coffee every now and then. She's happy to see him, she says. He's the only one, she says, who ever calls her Evelyn.

"We're fine," she tells her.

Though of course they aren't fine. They're light-years from fine. And there's a split second where she almost tells her that instead, where she almost says yes, get on that plane, come on, come babysit for me, what the hell. Their mother always said that Evvie had a big heart and she knows this to be true. Kids, friends, her cats and dogs—she has two of each, she recalls—all adore her. For a moment she almost feels—my god—lonely.

But an hour in her sister's care, an hour under the eye of her sincere regard will drive her nuts.

She'll get through this herself. She always has.

In the days that follow Pat watches it all, first from outside the room and then, in surgical mask and gown, from inside, and finally, from the plate-glass windows of the operating theatre, looking down at them from above.

She sees Delia's eyes flutter from within her bandages, hears her murmur in pain despite the drugs, sees nurses changing the dressings on her face, on her neck, her hands, on her unbroken arm, the arm swollen terribly and charred black, fluid leaking from its pores. Sees her reach up with the broken arm to her face as though the arm were whole and unharmed and watches the nurse, yet another nurse, restrain her and set it back in place.

On the evening of the second day Delia opens her eyes and searches around the room and her eyes find her mothers' eyes, her mother standing at a distance all in white, and she thinks how strange that must seem to her if she is truly aware of her at all.

She watches nurses change bedpans. Consult charts. Adjust the drips and replace the clear plastic bags above her head.

Through her own reflection in the window of the operating theatre she watches the process of debridement—such a funny word for such a procedure, *the unmaking of a bride*—watches them remove dead tissue from her head, neck, and arms. They can do such wonderful things with lasers these days.

And she is cognizant of a strange sense of detachment from all this, as though it were happening to some other daughter and some other mother and she were merely an observer from this privileged vantage point of their various machinations, both everyday and complex, a detachment which at first surprises her and then doesn't. Because it's to be expected. Courage is a trouper's middle name. Courage is what it takes, always. Courage and tough determination.

The text from Roman reads, *Producers want to speak with you personally. Told them, not possible. Send condolences but bottom line, say they have to move on. "Every day delayed money lost." Pricks.*

Pricks indeed. But that's to be expected too.

Early on the morning of the third day she steps out for a smoke and stands near an ash bin at the entrance to the building when she sees a van pull up beside her, and even before they hustle out the sliding doors—the photographer brandishing his video camera, the reporter her voice recorder—she can smell it on them.

Vultures.

Bart has warned her.

She tosses them the lit cigarette, showering sparks at the surprised photographer's feet before he can get off a single blessed frame and pushes through the revolving doors to the safety and frigid air inside.

"At least you don't hate me, do you girl?"

He slides open the glass door and watches her sidle meekly out onto the lawn, giving him a sidelong glance past the rim of her Cone of Shame—that's what Wiki calls it anyway, *dumb name*—and a slow wave of the tail. He can tell that despite his lubing her belly, chest, and legs down every morning and every night after dinner, she's still hurting.

He resists the urge to apologize to her yet again. He's apologizing to everybody these days. His mom. His dad. His sister—drugged, dead to the world. The cops.

His mom is stony.

He's told her twice how sorry he is. Or tried to. The first time was right after it happened. The second time in the hospital, standing at the observation window, watching Delia sleep. She said, *I know.* She might have said *uh-huh* or *yeah, right*—that was the way she said it. Like who cared if he was sorry. Like she was barely following him, barely even hearing him.

His dad's a little better. His dad just seems *distracted.* There's so much on his mind, he guesses. And he's not just distracted around him. When the two detectives arrived—*routine follow-up, they said*—he poured them coffee they didn't ask for. Asked them what they had under the hood of the squad car. When he led them upstairs to his room, to show them the rig that had caused the accident, and then to hers, to the burned bed, the destroyed, shattered dollhouse, when he explained to them what happened, it was as though he were some kind of museum tour guide and not the guy whose family this had all happened to and then when he, Robbie, had to confirm it all, go over every bit of it again, and when doing that brought him to tears, he couldn't help it, the tears just came, it was one of the cops who patted him on the shoulder and said, it's okay kid. It's okay.

Not his dad.

He didn't then. And he hasn't since either.

He watches his dog sniff around in the grass.

At least he isn't going to jail. The cops explained that much. That much is a relief at least.

The Cone of Shame.

Wrong dog, he thinks, wearing it.

Rain. Not yet, but soon. She can smell it in the air, hear it in the stillness, feel the cooling thickness in the air as it drifts across her shaven belly.

She is aware of a bite, an itch, constant, which proceeds from beneath her hind legs across her belly and chest down all four legs, prickly as she moves zigzag from swing set to slide and back again, her nose fully awake and drinking in the morning.

The small plastic protrusion from her neck is gone now and its former location bandaged but there is still that circular barrier, annoying in its flexive inflexibility, its being there, surrounding her head, preventing her from licking her wounds as she knows she ought to, magnifying sounds in front of her and dimming those behind. She can see no usefulness to this except to restrict and annoy her and wonders what she has done to be punished so.

She crouches to pee. Listens with satisfaction to her body's perfect function.

And there's that familiar scent. Over by the fence.

She can hear them now too.

She finishes her business and ambles over and there they are, the two gray kits, sniffing at the old fallen tree on the far side of the fence. At her approach their tiny ears point and tilt in her direction. She can smell their mother too now, heavy with scent, and locates her watching silent from the clump of brambles not twelve feet away. With her so near she approaches very slowly so as not to offend.

The kits sniff at her through a knot in the fence, small black noses poking at the hole as though in competition with each other.

We see this and smile. We want to play. But we're frustrated by the fence, by the cone, by the presence of the mother nearby. By the weakness in a body which only days ago could have run and climbed the slide, vaulted the fence, and joined them.

Still, this is a pretty sight.

Our fingers tighten on the sheets on the hospital bed and then release.

We watch the kits poke noses and then tiny paws through the knothole, trying to get to us, listen to their happy purring chirp.

The air grows heavy. Soon it will rain.

NINE

O n the third to last day of Delia's major surgery, her doctors
applying swaths of skin to her left arm—having previously
grafted it to their satisfaction to her face, neck, and head—
Robbie removes the cone.

He's that morning applied ointment to her burns as usual and
marveled at her patience with him. Coming home from school he's
thought about her moving listless through the house, feet twitching
as she sleeps, grunting as she raises herself up to a sitting position like
a dog twice her age, and decides she's had enough of the damn cone.
He might catch hell from his mom and dad.

He doesn't care.

They haven't said he couldn't.

She meets him at the door and looking up at him so sadly she
reinforces his resolve so he leads her to the kitchen and puts his books
down on the table and bends to her and pushes the tabs from the cone

through the punch-holes in her collar and pulls it away off her neck and releases her.

For a moment she just stands there blinking and then the tail starts to go and she begins walking round and round in circles, her head turning ahead of the rest of her as though she's looking for the thing which isn't there anymore thanks to him and he smiles.

It feels like the first real smile in a long time.

He lets her out to do her business and gathers up his books and turns toward the stairs and smells fresh paint and hears the voices as he climbs, hearty male voices—the painters Jeff and Barry who in private he's dubbed Ben and Jerry—and his father's. His mother is still at the hospital. As he enters the room his father is handing them cash and he can see they're preparing to leave, drop-clothes folded, paint cans stacked.

They say hi and he says hi and his father doesn't smile.

He goes to his room and closes the door. Tosses his books down on the bed. In his mind he replays that afternoon in the cafeteria, aware again of his classmates' eyes on him, their whispering.

It'd gone on like that off and on for days now.

He and his sister are *talked about*.

It's been on the evening news. The whole story, evidently. Only local but local was bad enough. Neither he nor his mom or dad have caught it but Roman has. He's recorded the thing and is sending it to them on disc. Some of the papers are carrying it too.

Plus Margot Dorsey has supposedly put it up on her Facebook page. He hasn't gone there. He isn't going to. Margot's always been a pain. Chased him all the way through the seventh grade. He'd like to shove those braces down her whiny throat.

Everybody's named names, of course. So that his own part in this is clear.

He's the kid who'd burned his sister.

He eats his lunch alone.

The dog's watching her as she slips on her shoes. The dog is minus her lampshade. She wonders when that has happened. The dog is still watching her when she changes her dress, which makes her uneasy somehow. Why the hell that should be she doesn't know. A pair of shoes. A dress. She's going out. She can't sit. She can't rest. So what?

The drive to Roman's takes a matter of minutes. He meets her at the doorstep and lets her inside and then kisses her more gently than she'd like, to be honest, when what she really wants is to be jolted out of her day, to be white-hot beneath him for the next hour or so while Bart does his banking and the shopping and Robbie is supposedly at his homework in his room and her daughter breathes in and out in her hospital bed oblivious to everything, to the disaster of her life, to the months ahead, so that she tears off his clothes there in the hallway and leads him naked by his cock into the bedroom and pushes him down on the bed and that's better, finally.

She's disappeared. She's gone.

Caity lies on Bart's easy chair, on which she has lately had permission to be. She'll take advantage while she can. The leather is cool and soothing on her belly. Robbie's on the couch, his fingers flying across his pad. Pat walks in through the front door, sighs, and removes her shoes. She doesn't say a word to either of them, passes them by to the kitchen. Caity hears a cupboard open, a glass set down, and bottle set down, the refrigerator door open, ice in the glass, and pouring. Pat sighs again.

Caity gets up off the chair, crosses the living room floor and clumps up the stairs and down the hall to Delia's room.

The room smells terrible and not like Delia's room at all but the window is open as she'd knew it would be and fresh air flows inside. She'd felt its steady flow across her belly all the way down the hall. It's an effort to pull herself up over the windowsill and onto the roof but it's worth it once she's out there.

There's her old weathered blanket. There's her toy.

She roots around in the blanket with her nose and scratches at it with her front paws until she's created a comfortable bed.

She looks up.

And we see the stars.

Bart sits at his desk. She paces back and forth in front of it.

"It'll go back up," he's saying. "It just takes time. We need more time."

"Excuse me? It went from forty dollars a share to five dollars a share in less than six months, Bart. How many did you buy?"

He won't look at her.

"Twenty thousand."

"What?"

"It was up to a hundred a share after two months, Pat. We were up a million fucking two!"

"And now you're down . . ."

"Seven hundred."

"*Thousand.* Seven hundred *thousand.* Jesus, Bart!"

"Hey, Chomp Chips checks are starting to come in. They'll keep us afloat on our monthly expenses if they keep running it, which you *know* they will. We'll be fine on property and federal next month. It's these goddamn hospital bills, Pat . . ."

"What do you mean? The hospital bills are co-pays. Not full amounts."

He shakes his head. "They're full amounts."

"What the hell are you talking about? We have insurance."

"No. We don't. I let it lapse. Delia was going to be upgraded once the show started. Who the hell knew."

She can't believe it. He calls himself a *business manager*? A father? A husband?

"Why you goddamn . . . you fucking *fry cook*!"

She can't find the words. Those will have to do.

"What did you call me?"

Oh, you're angry now, are you?

Poser. Amateur. Idiot.

She can't stand the look of him. She turns and stalks out of the room, slams the goddamn door behind her as hard as she goddamn can.

Fucking fry cook!

We dream.

We move back to the window, through the window. We're curious. We hear someone shouting, a door slam.

We move to the top of the stairs and down the stairs and here are all the people we know, all the important ones anyhow, and we taste anger and bewilderment. Anger from Bart and Patricia as they rush through the living room to the kitchen. Bewilderment from Robbie as he follows them paces behind. The first has the tang of sharp cold metal. The second a sweet thick foam.

"What did you say? What did you call me?" Bart shouts.

"You heard me!"

"You watch your mouth, woman! Dammit!"

Bart tears a bottle of gin from the cupboard. He unscrews and pours. We know the scent, we can read the bottle. Tanqueray.

Patricia pulls a pan off the row of them in various sizes which depend from hooks along the shelves. Shakes it at him.

"I called you a fry cook. *That's what you were when I met you, that's all you are and all you'll ever be!"*

She advances. He backs a step away.

Our fingers clutch the bedsheet. We're scared.

Robbie sits as though struck down.

"What the hell was I thinking? I knew I should have hired a manager. Hell, I should have just taken care of everything myself and left you to your toy cars and gizmos instead of letting a goddamn fry cook do a man's job."

"Hey. You just hold the fuck on there, Pat!"

"Why does she keep calling you a fry cook, dad?" says Robbie. We can barely hear him. We can smell the tightness in his bladder.

"Because that's what he was. What he is," says Pat. "Your mom's right out of college waitressing for the summer right? And Daddy Bart here's this big, strong, head-cook-slash-manager. And I was sooooo impressed!"

"Screw you, Pat." Bart drinks.

"It went belly-up before the summer was over."

She drops the pan into the empty sink. We flinch at the sound, it rings harsh in the air. She goes to the cupboard. Pours. The liquor is a light amber.

We can read the label. Glenfiddich.

A silence while she drinks, leaning against the counter. Bart stands motionless across from her. They are checkers on a checkerboard, each awaiting the next move.

"The doctors say that the major surgeries are over," he says. "The rest are just cosmetic. The bills won't be as bad as . . . we're going to be okay. We'll be okay."

She shakes her head. "No we won't, Bart. We're goddamn ruined. This has ruined us. Don't you see? Don't you get it?"

She places the glass down gently on the counter. Somehow the glass has gone empty. We must have been distracted. Perhaps by Robbie's left foot drumming against the floor. Perhaps by beeping from the corridor. Nurses rushing by.

"You're done," she says. "I'm taking over your office. The files, the checkbook, everything. Roman and I will figure out how to get us out of this mess."

She pushes away from the counter.

"First thing I'm doing is selling your fucking car."

She walks out of the room. We can hear her on the stairs. Robbie and Bart just look at one another for a moment.

We turn away. We curl up onto the easy chair. We nestle in as deeply as we can. We pull up a sheet. We wipe away a tear we were not aware was there.

Our bad dream is over.

Bart is seriously unprepared for what he's looking at. But then how could he not be? How could any of them possibly be prepared?

They're all here, seated around Delia's bed in a semicircle while Dr. Ludlow speaks to her in his quiet, steady voice. Robbie has taken the day off from school for this.

And in theory they're ready. Nicole, the doctor's nurse practitioner, has met with Pat the day before, given her prescriptions to fill at the hospital pharmacy, handed her the ointments, tubes, and jars they'll need. After that she'd seen the physical therapist. Been given a rundown of the necessary exercises—how to handle her daughter's body, how much is good for her and how often and what's not good for her at all. Together they've seen the dietician and have a list of purchases to make, a list of dos and don'ts foodwise.

They're all set.

Still they're nervous about this. All of them. That much is obvious. He can easily read his wife and son. Pat's arms are crossed tight across her chest. Her *I'm holding it all inside position*. Robbie's leaning forward, his elbows on his knees, white-knuckled hands clasped together. Bart rolls his neck and shoulders against his own tension and feels them crack.

Only Delia seems unfazed. She sits up against the pillows and simply listens.

"As you know this has been quite a lengthy process," Ludlow's saying, "and there's still a long road ahead, cosmetically speaking. But the important part's over. With proper homecare, Delia will be fine, strong, and healthy."

The doctor turns to her. "You're going home, Delia. *Finally*, right? You get out of here! You get to sleep in your own room again, your own bed. Excited about that?"

"Not really," she says.

He laughs. "Why not?"

"There's ghosts in there. In my room. They did this to me. Ghosts did."

Beside him Robbie groans.

Ludlow looks at Pat and then at him. He feels his face flush. No, they haven't told her. *That it was her brother's doing.*

"Are there now," the doctor says.

"No," Pat's voice is very small. "It wasn't ghosts, Delia. It was never ghosts. It was . . ."

He reaches out and gently squeezes his wife's arm. *Don't go there,* the squeeze says. *Not now.*

"It was what, mom?"

Pat gets it. *Don't go there.*

ALAMEDA FREE LIBRARY

"Doctor?" she says.

And Ludlow gets it too. *Change the subject.*

"Yes. Okay," he says and pulls his surgical mask up over his face. "Let's have a look, shall we? Lie back. Close your eyes. Now keep in mind that there's still swelling taking place and will be for a while, but that will fade . . ."

And that's when Bart begins to tune him out, as Delia closes her eyes and he cuts away the bandages from her face and she lies there revealed, his beautiful young daughter turned into a patchwork of flesh, grafts the color of meat extending down from the top of her hairless head to the sides of her cheeks in front of her ears, over the melted ears themselves into the flesh of her neck, then down her forehead to just above her eyes, those precious eyes that were protected by her hands as she pressed them to her face, her skin whole and untouched across sickly pale cheeks which had been protected too by those hands, and then more raw grafting across the tip of her nose and chin because those same small hands did not suffice and had left them bare to the singe of flames.

My god.

He is looking at the clear imprint of two hands splayed across her face.

Ghostly thin fingers reaching up from her eyes into what had been her hairline, outlined in angry red.

Those hands which had saved her, now disfigure her.

He remembers to breathe.

He is glad her eyes are closed. Glad she can't see him.

He'll have to work on that. Put his game face on from here on in. He can do that. He'll have to.

She's coming home.

ALAMEDA FREE LIBRARY

TEN

Delia's still a little woozy from whatever they have her on so that when she stands while Robbie ditches the wheelchair she takes mom's arm waiting for dad to bring the car around, and then Robbie's on the other side of her so she takes hold of his arm too, and it's a little while before she realizes that they're pretty much surrounded out there.

The news has gotten around.

Reporters and cameramen, circling her like bees. *Buzzing, buzzing.*

She pulls the red hoodie further up over her head.

"*Mrs. Cross? Congratulations on Delia's release . . .*"

"*Where's the dog? Where's Caity?*"

"*Yeah, we were expecting a reunion!*"

"*How you feeling, Delia? And you must be Robbie . . .*"

Dad gets out of the car and it's like in the movies, like she's a celebrity, him striding up to her and guiding her to the curb, arms held out to them waving them away like some Secret Service guy while Rob and her mom block them on either side and *how do they know Caity's name?* she wonders.

She's aware of her mom and dad asking them to back off, to leave them alone please. To please respect their privacy.

"Can we get a shot of the whole family together?"

"Are you going back to work again?"

They aren't listening. They're pushing and shoving. A dozen of them maybe. She doesn't know. She just drifts toward the car.

"I asked you nicely," says her mom and she almost doesn't recognize her voice, the voice is so mad. Her grip so tight on her arm it almost hurt. "But if that's not good enough then how about this? Get the *fuck* out of our way before I shove those cameras through your goddamn teeth!"

"But this is a wonderful story, Mrs. Cross . . . please . . ."

Dad pulls open the passenger side doors in front and back and Robbie gets in back and holds out his arms to her while mom moves her inside and slams the door and then gets in the front and slams that door too, and as her dad is making his way to the driver's side she sees one of the reporters step right in front of him and for a moment she thinks her dad's going to hit him, he's so angry but then he stops and listens instead. She's started to roll up the window but then she stops and listens too.

"These other guys are animals, freeloaders," the man is saying, "but my station will *pay* for your story, Mr. Cross." He hands dad a card. The reporter smiles. "Way to knock down all those hospital bills, right?"

Her dad grunts something and pockets the card and slides in behind the wheel. The car's already running so he throws it into gear and they pull away.

"Fucking ambulance chasers! What the hell kind of people would . . . ?"

"Dad," she says. "It's okay, dad. They just want to hear about me and Caity."

She leans forward and puts a hand on his shoulder. Feels the trembling slowly stop.

Then after that they drive in silence.

She's aware of them long before she hears them, smells them, sees them. They're coming home.

All of them.

She climbs up on the chair by the window and gazes out but it's still too early, it'll be a while yet and the chair can't contain her so she jumps back down to the floor and her tail is going, her butt's going—wiggle-butt, wiggle-butt her memory says to her—and her whimpered voice sounds joyous and scared to her ears as she circles round and round.

When the car pulls up she goes back up to the chair again and there they are out the window, getting out and walking toward the house, toward her, Delia is walking toward her and her whole body is shaking with excitement now and she can smell them, each of them, over and beyond the car-smells, the smell of fresh-mown grass, she can identify each footfall. She hears Delia's steps more hesitant than she's used to. Pat's crisp. Bart's plodding.

The lock disengages and the door opens and she navigates perfectly between Bart's legs and Robbie's to Delia's, ignoring Pat beside her. And then she's up on her hind legs pawing at Delia's legs and Robbie reaches down, ruffles her back, shifts her gently away.

"Down, Caits," he says, "calm down. She's still hurt . . . just like you . . ."

Delia laughs. "That's my girl," she says, reaching out to pet her. "I missed you, Caiters. Oh, I missed you, girl!"

Pat moves her toward the sofa and eases her down and then the open lap is there so she hops up and lays her front paws and head across it as Delia embraces her and pulls her toward her for a long hug and a kiss. Many kisses. A squeal of contentment rises and escapes from her throat. She licks her drooling lips. The hoodie falls away down across Delia's shoulders and she looks up and sees her face, sniffs at it.

Strange.
Delia's face but not.
No, Delia's face all right. Hers. Delia's.
Who smiles and giggles as she licks it and licks it with her warm wet tongue.
And here we are.

Robbie wonders how she feels, sitting there at the dinner table after all this time. Like normal. Like nothing's happened at all. He can't tell. He's never been able to figure his sister. Just doing what she did, performing, getting up in front of a bunch of people and actually *liking* it. When Robbie has to read out loud in class it takes all he can do not to run out of the room screaming.

And here she is, Caity's head resting on her lap while she forks up some fried zucchini, everybody silent at the table which is weird enough right there, never mind that Caity is the only one who seems to be able to look at her, at her ruined face. Mom and dad aren't even making an effort, not even just for show. Dad's pushing around his mashed potatoes while he reads the paper. Mom's nursing her Bloody Mary. She hasn't even touched her steak.

It isn't right. She's not some freak. They should be looking.

He remembers his sister's tastes. There's a piece of steak on the platter that looks just right for her. He forks it up.

"Hey, sis," he says, "you want the crispy one?"

She looks at him real serious-like and he right away realizes his blunder. Crispy? *Burned?* Awww, shit!

He wants to say something, to take it back somehow—thinking how could I be so *stupid?*—but she just keeps looking at him wide-eyed like she can't believe what he's said either and then her mouth turns up and she's grinning and the next thing he knows they're both busted up laughing while mom and dad just sit there looked at the two nut-cases across the table.

But it's good. It breaks the tension at least for a while and after-ward they watch *Birdman* for the third time—dad's Netflixed it, a good choice because it's a favorite of everybody's—and when Delia asks what happened to the new TV because they're watching the old one, dad doesn't even blink an eye, just says *we didn't need it* and that's that.

Then mom wants them to get ready for bed.

"Can I sleep out here tonight?" Delia asks. Like she's still afraid of something up there.

"Not a good idea, hon," says his mom. "You need some solid rest. And your room's all fixed up now."

"Good as new," says dad. "Better."

But Delia shifts, uneasy on the couch, and that's when the phone rings. Mom gets up to answer it.

"Robbie you'll deal with Caity, right?" his dad says.

"Sure, dad."

"Caity?" Delia asks.

"There's this cream stuff. For where she's hurt," Robbie says.

"I can do it."

"You don't know how yet. I'll do it tonight and show you how in the morning, okay?"

"All right."

"None of your goddamn business!" his mom says into the phone. They all look up at her, startled.

"Kids? Upstairs," his dad says. It isn't a request.

They head for the stairs.

Is this Mrs. Cross? the man said. And she said yes. And he said, *how's Delia? How's she adjusting to home life?* Which was when she blew it.

"None of your goddamn business! Who is this?"

"Pardon me, ma'am. I'm Brian Bishop with FFMN InfoCorp . . ."

"FFMN? Listen . . ."

"I talked with your husband. Mrs. Cross, please hear me out. Delia and her dog . . . her *hero* dog . . . we'd all of us just love to . . ."

She slams down the receiver. Bart is beside her. He puts a hand on her shoulder. She shrugs it off. She's fuming.

"Hey, just don't answer the phone for a while anymore, okay?" he says. "Let me handle it."

"Do you think *they* think about what we're going through? Do you think they *care?* FFMN. Fucking assholes . . ."

"Babe . . ."

"If they call back, you go ahead. Answer. Ask them if they know what it feels like to see everything . . . something . . . someone they love get . . ."

He puts his arms around her and this time she lets him. He leads her to the couch.

"She's going to be okay, hon . . ."

The anger flares. "And what about the rest of us, Bart? You? Me? Robbie?"

He breaks away and looks at her for a long moment, seems to be thinking. Then digs a card out of his shirt pocket. He flicks it with his index finger.

"What?"

He says nothing. Just keeps flicking at the card. On top of everything else it's just plain irritating. *Quit it*, she thinks. For god's sake. *Flick, flick . . .*

From the top of the stairs we hear it. We hear it too standing in our bathroom, gazing into the mirror. Flick, flick. We sit immobile at the stairs' summit, silent. We gaze at our reflection in the mirror. Our ears perk up. We listen to them down below.

"*FFMM,*" *he says.*

"*Yes? So?*"

"*That's a big outfit, Pat. All I'm saying . . .*"

"*What exactly are you saying? Stop it with the card, will you?*"

"*All right. Consider this. They'll pay.*"

"*What are you talking about?*"

We brush our teeth. Careful of our damaged lips. We continue listening.

"*For the story, Pat. For Delia. Caity. What happened. They'll pay. Possibly a lot. Diane Fleet, Hotline. Think about it.*"

We hear a pause, feel him assertive and feel her falter. She shakes her head, a tiny rustle. She sighs.

"I've got to go take care of Delia," she says. "Do me a favor and tomorrow find her a new tutor, will you? One, not half a dozen. One we can afford."

She rises off the sofa. We climb into bed. We wait.

Her mom is rubbing this thick creamy stuff into her forehead.

"Does that hurt?" she asks.

"No." It feels good in fact. Cool against her skin.

Mom dips her hand into the cream, rubs it into the back of her neck. That feels good too.

"You're a brave girl," she says. "You remind me of *my* mom, before . . ."

"Before the accident, right? Before she . . . started drinking?"

This is dangerous territory, she knows. They don't talk about her grandma much.

"Yes. You know that I was about your age when my dad . . ."

"Yeah."

"So between that and the osteoporosis . . ."

"Bad bones."

"Yes, bad bones."

"Are my bones bad?"

"No. Your bones are strong."

"Why do I remind you of her?"

"Because before the accident, no matter how much she hurt, her eyes were always steady, strong. The way she looked at you. Always . . . certain. Your eyes are strong, like hers."

"You think so?"

"Yeah. I do."

"It's weird, mom. My eyes. I feel like I can *see* better now than before, in a way."

"Really? What do you mean?"

How can she tell her? She isn't even sure herself. Only that it's true.

"I don't know. Everything's different. Every*body*. It's not the same. It's different."

We're different.

She stops rubbing and stares at her daughter, at her daughter's ravaged face gleaming beneath the thin coat of cream. Delia stares back. Delia's stare makes her uncomfortable. Why has she begun this conversation? She doesn't like it. Doesn't like where it's going. She has this ridiculous feeling. It's like her daughter could see into *her* just now, at just this very moment, right down deep into her soul. Those parts of her, maybe, that were her mother's daughter. Not her favorite parts. Was that what she meant?

Just who and what is she seeing?

The cream feels silky on her fingertips. She continues rubbing, careful against her daughter's tender skin.

"All done, girl. Come on."

He walks her over to Delia's room, knocks once, and enters.

"You guys finished? We're finished."

"Yeah, us too," Delia says.

She closes the book on her lap and Caity jumps onto the bed and curls up in its place.

Robbie sits down next to her. Bounces a little, tested the springs on the new bed.

"Pretty good," he says. "What do you think?"

His gesture encompasses the room. The walls had been pink. He'd never thought much of that. Now it was a simple cream. Much better, he thinks. His is still the same pastel blue as when he was a kid.

"It's okay," she says.

Her voice says it isn't.

He stops bouncing. "Yeah? So? What's up? You want to talk about it?"

"I'm scared, Rob."

"Scared of what?"

"You think the ghosts went away? With the fire?"

Damn. They *still* haven't told her. He can't believe it. Why would they . . . *leave it up to him? Why couldn't they have . . . ?*

Damn!

"It wasn't ghosts, Delia. There aren't any ghosts. Never were."

"You're trying to make me feel better."

He doesn't want to cry. He can feel their eyes on him. Hers and Caity's too.

"It was me, Deal. God! I'm so sorry. I'm really, really . . ."

And then the tears do come.

He tells her everything.

Patricia stands in the dark, in the doorway. Apart from her, the house is asleep.

As her eyes accustom gradually to the darkness she watches her daughter sleep, Caity beside her. The rise and fall of their bodies as they breathe. Her daughter's sweet face—in the dimness, that face undamaged, whole, unscarred. All gentle planes and angles.

Her hand goes to her own face, her lips, her cheekbones, her brow. Flawless, perfect.

She thinks, how can this be.

She stands a long while, listening to her own breathing. In time, a synchronicity between her daughter's breathing and her own. In this they are together. In this moment they are a match. The dog's breath coming faster than theirs, her heart pumping faster, pumping blood which is alien to them.

Yet the dog has saved her life.

The hero dog.

She reaches down and touches her breasts. With these she nursed her baby. She had been an easy baby. Full of life.

Her baby still. *Remember that. Keep that in mind.*

You have a duty here. Yes.

The dog's eyes are open and glint in the thin skein of night.

She walks downstairs to the telephone on the island bar. Hits the button for recent calls and then the most recent.

Brian Bishop. FFMN.

She pours herself a short scotch and writes down the number to call tomorrow and by the time the drink is finished has already composed exactly what she wants to say.

ELEVEN

It's not the same. A Green Room is a Green Room she supposes, with the familiar table of snacks and bottled drinks, the mirrored wall in front of her lined with brushes, combs, makeup, tissues and all that stuff, the rack of clothes, the too-bright lights. She'd been in them dozens of times but this is different somehow. She doesn't feel like a star. She doesn't even feel like a performer. What's she doing here? She watches the grips and stagehands come and go and tries to settle deep into her oversized lounger, disappear into her red hoodie. Just disappear.

Her mom seems fine with all of it. Standing by the door talking to this guy John Latoya, the anchor-slash-producer who she's yet to meet, talking as though it were any other shoot in the world, Fruity Fingers or Chomp Chips or whatever. And maybe that's the way she ought to think about it, just any old shoot, just another job.

But it feels weird. They're going to talk about *her*. She isn't *playing somebody*. She's supposed to be herself. *Just be yourself, honey,* her mom said. Nobody's ever asked her to do *that* before.

When her mom and the anchor guy walk over she wraps her hand twice around Caity's leash so that she's just that much closer to her and she feels just that much more secure.

"How you ladies doing this morning?" Latoya says.

Big smile. *At least the teeth are real,* she thinks. He's one of those people, she can already tell, who speaks to kids like they're all in the first grade. There are paper towels sticking up out of his collar to keep the makeup from messing up his baby-blue shirt and blue-and-red striped tie.

"Delia, this is John," her mom says. "He's going to be interviewing us."

John sticks out his bony hand and she shakes it.

"Pleased to meetcha," he says. "Did you get to try any of those *donuts*? I like the *sprinkly ones* myself."

Her mom pulls her cell phone out of her pocket and reads the text.

"It's Roman," she says. "Could you excuse me a moment?"

"Of course," John says.

She punches in the number and walks off into a corner. John kneels down to Delia's level. Tries to peer under her hoodie. She has her head down so he isn't having much luck. He smells of cologne and hair stuff. Beside her she can feel Caity tense. The cologne and hair stuff probably offend her. She can't blame her. Neither of them, it seems, are going to be instantly nuts about this guy.

John seems oblivious. He reaches over and ruffles Caity's head. Her ears go flat. He doesn't notice this either.

"So, how long have you two been *buddies*?" he says, agreeably enough.

"Since I got her."

"When was that?"

"Two years ago. She'll be three in November."

"I see. So you've been friends a *good long time*, then."

She raises her head. Looks at him.

"How come you want me and Caity on your show?"

The smile gets bigger but she can tell she's caught him off guard.

"That's a *very good* question," he says. "Why do I want you on my *show.* Well, it's not every day a girl's dog saves her *life,* is it?" He turns to Caity. "*Is it,* old girl?"

He ruffles the hair on her neck. She flinches.

"It's the kind of story that *inspires* people, Delia. You two—your friendship and what you've *gone through* together—that's inspiring stuff! It makes people *feel* good. You can understand *that,* can't you?"

Well, duh, she thinks.

"But we got hurt," she says.

"Yes. Yes, you did. You *got hurt.* But you're *alive.* And isn't that amazing?"

He reaches out to pat Caity on the shoulder but Caity's had enough. She lets out a low growl. Just enough so John can hear. He pulls his hand away. "She's not used to you," Delia says.

"I . . . sure," he says.

He stands. *Keep that dog away from me,* his face tells her. She has to repress a smile. He reminds her of Roman.

"Well. We'll see you shortly then, right? Pleasure to meet the both of you. You're going to be just great. Just *be yourself.*"

He turns and walks away and as though on cue he's surrounded by staff asking questions, taking instructions. Delia's instantly forgotten. And to her, that's just fine. Her mom appears behind them, finishing up her phone call.

"Perfect," she says. "Sign on my behalf. Send me a copy. Transfer the funds to *my* Delia account. Not Bart's. Thanks, Roman."

She clicks the phone off and sits down next to Delia. Puts her arm around her. Even with her mom there she still feels uncomfortable.

"Are there . . . sides or anything?" she asks.

"No, honey. You just say what you want to say."

"Like what?"

She sighs. "This isn't acting, kiddo. This is just talking. Just listen to the questions and answer them. You'll get the hang of it right away. You'll see. Just . . ."

"I know. *Just be yourself.*"

They sit down in the cushy interview armchairs, Pat's nearest where John's going to sit and Delia beside her with Caity nestled between her knees. The stage set is your basic faux-All-American living room, coffee table in front of them, fake flowers in a vase on the table, framed prints on the walls, bookshelves, throw rugs, windows leading to nowhere.

Pat thinks, *talk about mixed emotions.* Good god.

She's on a set. Not between, before, or after takes this time—a total first for her—with the purpose of actually *being on TV.* Live TV at that. She has no illusions. She's there to perform. To sell this thing. Or rather to sell it further since Roman is already depositing the check from FFMM in her company account. And a goodly check at that. But she's looking down the road. If they get this right maybe other gigs will follow. Even if it's small-time stuff they need the money. She's here to make this work. In that she is determined.

But she's also scared as hell that it won't work at all. That any one of a thousand things could go wrong and screw the pooch entirely. A single moment. A single misstep. So much seems outside her control. It was *live fucking TV!* She could come off wrong somehow or Delia could or Caity could shit the goddamn fake oriental rug.

Already she is sweating. The big soft-box lighting is pouring out tons of heat. Where was makeup when you needed them?

And where the hell is Bart? He's supposed to have been here half an hour ago. Where was your support when you needed it?

Ed Cullen, the director, is sweating too and he isn't even under these lights. He walks over and introduces himself and they shake hands.

"I'm wondering if we can't have Caity sit to the side for the first part of the interview," he says. "Would that be all right?"

"Why?" Delia says. "I thought . . ."

She cuts her daughter off. They know what they want. "Sure," she says. "No problem. Do you have someone who . . . ?"

As if by magic a pretty young girl in headphones appears behind him. A production assistant. You could always tell them by the combination of brisk efficiency and out-and-out fluster.

"Hi, I'm Bianca," she says. "Okay if I watch Caity for a little while, Delia?"

Delia peers out from under the red hood, her eyes in shadow.

"I don't know you," she says.

The PA's smiling but she's also tense, twisting at her belt loop with her fingers.

Her daughter is being difficult.

The hell she is.

"Delia."

It's a fucking command and she takes it as such.

"I'll take good care of her," the PA says. "I promise."

Delia points to behind the stage-left camera.

"You want her over there?"

The girl smiles. "It's as good a place as any. Just for the first segment, okay?"

Delia looks down at Caity, tilts the dog's head upward so that they're eye to eye for a moment and then releases her and inclines her head stage left. Caity stands and walks solemnly behind the camera, leash trailing. The young PA is impressed.

"I'd say she listens well," she says. "But you didn't say anything!"

The girl walks over and picks up the leash and rustles the fur along Caity's neck and then John steps onstage and sits down smiling and she forgets about the dog because there's makeup at last, a woman dabbing at John's face and another at hers which feels wonderful but when hers is finished and the woman bends down to do touch-up on Delia, Pat stops her.

"She's fine," she says.

That face is not going to be touched. No way.

"Okay, ladies," John says. "Do you have any questions before we start?"

She doesn't. She's ready.

They mike them each and a few minutes later the countdown begins.

Fucking 405. He's been creeping along staring up at the SUNSET BLVD., WILSHIRE BLVD., SANTA MONICA BLVD. signs overhead and at the Getty Museum in the distance for twenty minutes now before traffic starts moving again. Fucking hellhole of a triangulation. And now he is three-quarters of an hour late and his wife and daughter are up there onstage already.

The meeting with his guy at Wells Fargo had been pretty good, if a bit depressing by its very nature. Their credit's still good. So either a home equity loan or a home equity line of credit seems equally doable. He's leaning toward the credit line rather than the lump sum but he'll have to discuss that with Pat.

Thank god they have the house. Without the house right now he didn't know where they'd be.

He catches Pat's eye and waves and she nods. So at least she knows he's there. He sees Caity on a leash with some girl behind camera three. Then they're on.

"So what goes through a mother's mind when something like this happens?"

John's voice has that same familiar intimate tone Pat recognizes from so many talking heads over the years. Was there some school for this somewhere? Classes in intimate-concern-speak? Legs crossed, he leans in close.

His cologne wafts over.

"God," she says. "I've never been so scared in my life."

"I can imagine."

No you can't. He leans in closer.

"Tell me. What caused the fire in the first place, Pat?"

"It was an accident, John. Faulty wiring in Delia's room. In her dollhouse. My dollhouse, actually. A present from my mother."

"I see. So, the fire starts, and what happens next?"

"Our son started yelling for us from upstairs . . ."

"That would be Delia's twin brother, Robbie, correct?"

"That's right."

"The police questioned Robbie, didn't they."

"Yes they did. He laid the wiring. He thought of it as a kind of present, a surprise. Lights in the dollhouse, you know? Robbie's just a boy. He didn't think. He didn't know any better. Not his fault."

The glance at her daughter is knee-jerk, involuntary. She hopes Delia's look of surprise at this series of lies doesn't register on camera. Delia's keeping her head down so she doubts it.

"Delia?" says John. "You realize you're a very lucky girl to be alive right now, don't you?"

"Yes. I do."

"And the reason you're alive is . . . ?"

"Caity. My dog . . . Caity."

She's practically mumbling. *Come on*, she thinks. I've taught you better than this, dammit.

"So, is there anything you'd like to tell us about your friend Caity before we bring her out here?"

Delia shrugs. Essays a small shy smile from underneath the hood. Would the camera hopefully pick *that* up? That smile?

She counts about three seconds of dead air. On television, three seconds is a fucking eternity.

"John, I think if you just . . ." Pat nods in the dog's direction.

He's good. He picks up on it right away.

"Sure. Even better. Let's just cut to the chase and meet the hero of our story. Delia's dog, Caity!"

The director cues Bianca, who puts on her best smile and begins to lead Caity onto the set but Caity needs no leading. Caity leads *her*. Directly over to John. Who is pretty damn taken aback when she sniffs him directly in the crotch and then trots over to Delia and sits between her knees.

"Well," says John, "that's one way to make friends, I guess." His smile is almost, but not quite, genuine.

John doesn't like dogs, she thinks. She'll shoot for a more simpatico interviewer next time. If there is a next time.

Caity raises her head to Delia, giving the camera a perfect view of the burns beneath her neck and chest. *Good dog*, she thinks.

"I guess Caity here's your hero isn't she, Delia?"

She shrugs and smiles again and strokes Caity's head.

Not good. What's with this shrugging? Not good at all.

"Delia?" she prompts.

"She's always been my hero."

"Is that right? How so?"

Delia just blinks at him like he's from outer space or something.

So that then John looks over to Pat as though to say, *do something, will you?* But if her goddamn daughter doesn't want to talk what is she supposed to do about it? She'll give her holy hell later, that's for damn sure. But right now? In front of the cameras? Nothing.

Delia stops petting her dog, lets her hand rest on Caity's shoulder. Then raises her head up full into the lights for the very first time. Though most of her face is still in shadow.

"You're not asking me what you really want to ask me," she says. "Why is that?"

"I'm . . . I'm not?"

"I don't think so."

He seems to think this over. Smiles, then goes serious again. But no *faux-face* this time. Serious.

"Well . . ."

"Yes?"

"You're right, Delia. There is something, but it's completely understandable if you don't want to . . ."

"Just ask."

He takes a deep breath.

"I think our viewers would want to know . . . the extent of . . ."

"Yes?"

"Could you take the hood down?"

"No."

And he wasn't expecting that. Hell, neither was she. *What kind of game are you playing here, Delia?*

"No?"

"No."

"Are you . . . shy?"

"No."

"Are you embarrassed? There's no need to be embarrassed."

"No. I'm not embarrassed."

"I won't press it . . . I mean, I understand. You've gone through an awful lot for someone your age . . ."

"Everybody's gone through bad stuff. It doesn't keep tomorrow from being better."

John's eyes flicker. He straightens in his chair. He sees an out, she thinks. He smells a way to save this.

"*'It doesn't keep tomorrow from being better.'* Those are brave words from a . . ."

"I don't want to because of you."

"Because of . . . me?"

"Yeah."

"What do you mean?"

"I don't want to scare you. My face would scare you."

"No, Delia. Nothing could be further from the truth. I think you're . . ."

Wonderful? Was he about to trip up and say *wonderful?* And would he really be meaning it?

"It's okay, John. It's all right. It's okay to be afraid."

He's showing now. Really showing. She's amazed. Delia's right. He *is* afraid to gaze at this head-on, under the lights. The harsh, unforgiving lights. She can read the ambivalence now with which he must have approached this from the get-go. This is not an interview he'd wanted to do. The very idea makes him uncomfortable. *Something in his past*, she thinks. Who knows what? But he's a pro. He'll get through it the way he always does. She feels an unexpected sympathy for the man.

It comes and goes. This man still has to be of use to them.

He looks down at Caity for a moment, who's staring at him, immobile, as though she were reading him too, and then back to Delia.

"You're sure?" she says.

And now John is smiling again and this time it's wholly real. Like he's almost glad to be found out.

He nods.

She turns fully into the lights. Directly into her hot-spot just as she's been taught to do.

She pulls down the hood.

And Pat could easily applaud her right then and there.

"This is me, Delia," she says. "This is who I am. This is me."

PART TWO

TWELVE

*T*his *Manny Choi*, she thinks, *this guy is a one-man circus.*

They're watching him on the big sixty-five-inch 4K Ultra High Definition TV monitor—*Bart would love this!* she thinks—as she pours herself a second modest glass of wine and sets the bottle back in its ice bucket amid the huge spread of food and drink arranged along the immaculate linen-covered Green Room table.

Following the opening splash they were running clips from the show. Newly assembled, she's learned, every day. Intercut with stock shots of the audience, laughing, dancing in the aisles, looking shocked, then hysterical, laughing even more. And there's Manny—our bright-faced, fifty-three-year-old Korean-American host—dancing amid a crowd of two-or-three-year-olds, displaying even less rhythm than the babies. Manny deadpanning a pretty fair Jack Benny as some woman shoots Silly String all over his face. Manny walking on his hands, crashing feet-first into the camera.

The audience is howling. While the announcer intones *Today on Choi and Company, with your host . . . Manny Choi!* and Manny's face appears peering like a thief from behind a curtain . . . *with everyone's favorite hunky handyman, Steeeve Keltin!* . . . and there's Steve, shot in fast-motion, tacking down an entire side of shingle roofing . . . *and world-renowned sword-swallower Annie Rosette!* . . . and Annie, sliding a sword from her throat, which immediately bursts into flame.

For a moment the screen goes black and then these little animated flowers bloom all around with puppy and kitten faces inside them the essence of cute and the music goes from pop to sweet . . . *and with the help of our sponsors, Innocina Brands and Spot-Clear Paper, a very* special *guest, along with her heroic best friend, here to inspire joy and wonder in all of us, just exactly as it did with . . .*

. . . Maaaaaaaaaaannnnnneeeeee!!! Choi!!!

My god, she thinks. *He's riding a fucking tricycle.*

Which he is. And licking an oversized lollipop. On the screen behind him is a photoshop blowup of his face plastered onto a baby goat in a bathtub. The meaning of which is utterly lost on her.

But the audience is laughing like crazy. While Manny pretends confusion, like he hasn't the foggiest notion why.

And this goonie-bird's daytime ratings are right up there with *Ellen's*, she thinks. High enough so that they paid top dollar.

What an amazing country this truly is.

He stands and waves and kicks the tricycle into the wings. The photo disappears.

"Awwww . . . thank you," he says, "or as we say in my former homeland . . ."

He cups a hand to his ear. The crowd knows the cue. Everyone joins in.

"Gamsahabnida!"

Applause. Choi bows and shakes his head.

"Wow, wow, wowwowwow. You ever notice when Americans try to say 'thank you' in Korean, it sounds like they're sneezing?"

He mimics a sneeze.

"Gam . . . gam . . . *gamsahbnida!*"

She checks out her daughter. Wondering how she's taking all this. Pat has seen the Choi show many times by now, doing her home- work, but Delia hasn't. She's watching the screen intently, nibbling a chicken nugget. She seems . . . interested. Not alarmed, at least. She isn't fleeing for the door.

"Your ears pop yet?" she says.

The descent into JFK had been abrupt.

"Not yet."

"Want some gum?" She has some in her purse. Forearmed, as always.

"Unh-unh. No thanks."

They watch in silence. As Manny does some of his catch-bits.

I Got Skillz.

With a volunteer from the audience who says she can dislocate her shoulder and then does, Manny going through all sorts of physical contortions—he's a pretty good physical comedian, actually—before giving up and stuffing some fake prize money into her shirt pocket.

Tweet Beat.

Wherein he's handed a tweet supposedly from one braidsuckler21— "*you mean to tell me there are at least twenty more people out there suckling braids?*" and proceeds to pick up a small Raggedy Ann doll from behind the couch—it's another living-room set, only cartoon-gaudy this time, with all the furnishings exaggerated and oversized. He starts sucking on one of its braids, seeming to find delight in doing so, and when he sets it back down and smiles there's a big string of red yarn stuck between his teeth.

The audience loves it.

He picks the strand from his teeth, drops it to the floor and reads another tweet. "'Congrats on Emmy nods. Pull down your pants and celebrate.' Well . . ." At which point dance music comes on and Manny's boogying, much more coordinated than with the two-year- olds in the clip, his pants slowly sliding off his hips until they pool down to the floor and he's dancing with his back to the audience in a pair of heart-embroidered boxers.

The audience loves that one *to death*.

"Whew!" he says, puffing. "Who knew pulling your pants down was such good cardio?"

Cheers and applause.

He waves. "Thanks, everybody!"

She watches Delia feed Caity a bite of chicken. Not fazed by this one bit, she thinks.

That's my girl.

The door opens and the AD leans inside.

"Places, ladies," he says.

It's a little past midnight Thursday morning before they all get to sit down in front of their old sixteen-inch Samsung to watch the show, routed through Bart's computer via AirPlay, a private link, password protected.

It won't air nationwide until three that afternoon and Bart's anxious, he has no idea what to expect. Pat had called him from the studio as promised once the taping was over around noon their time, nine in the morning his, but to his first and only question, *Well? How did it go?* all he got was *It was interesting, you'll see,* and he couldn't read her tone whatsoever. As though she wasn't sure herself. Which wasn't like his wife one bit.

They're tired, all of them, even Caity, who'd flown like a champ according to Pat, lying between Delia's legs for most of the five-and-a-half-hour flight rather than in cargo because Pat had had the presence of mind to register her as a service dog under the Americans with Disabilities Act, claiming Delia was a victim of PTSD. Impossible to debate. She lies on the couch between Delia and Robbie now, looking beat.

They fast-forward through Manny Choi's opening shenanigans right to the meat of things. Choi's settled into one of the three oversized easy chairs in front of the obligatory coffee table and is leaning in to the camera.

"Enough of the silly silly," he's saying, "let's switch gears to important things. Not that laughing isn't important. But sometimes we need to take a step back and focus on some of the harsh realities of life that are all too easy to ignore between our . . . mocha frappés."

Titters from the audience.

"Statistics say that, on average, in the United States, someone dies in a fire every 169 minutes and someone is injured every 30 minutes. Eighty-five percent of those fire deaths occur in homes.

"Our next guests are two survivors of these horrible statistics. Two friends who will be forever bonded because of a random accident that could have happened to any one of us, in any one of our homes. As you know, I have three gorgeous daughters. And more pets than your average zoo. So when I saw John Latoya's interview with these two last week, it hit me hard, believe me.

"Roll the tape, will you please?"

And he is more than familiar with this, of course, though he hasn't seen this edit, these cuts, or heard Latoya's overdubs. But there's Delia in her red hoodie, her eyes bathed in shadows.

"Could you take the hood down? Show us how this has changed you? I know it might be embarrassing, but I'm thinking we might be able to send a message to people about how important fire safety is in the home."

"I'm not embarrassed. I don't want to scare you."

Then a pause, camera on Latoya, slowly nodding.

"You're sure?"

Then on Delia, claiming the moment, pulling away the hoodie.

"This is me, Delia. This is who I am. This is me."

The clip ends and the camera returns to Manny Choi.

"Please welcome . . . Delia Cross, her mother, Patricia, and . . . their amazing dog . . . Caity."

He watches them cross the stage, Delia in a yellow hoodie this time and holding Caity's leash, Choi leaning in to kiss each of them and whisper something, everybody smiling, Choi stopping to slow-salute Caity and Caity dipping her head to him in her own kind of salute and then barking once, bright and loud and sharp, as though trained for this, as though she's done this every day.

"I'll be damned," Bart says. He glances over at Pat.

"I know," she says. "She's something, isn't she."

The audience is applauding wildly. Choi motions them to their chairs.

"Hwan-yeong," he says. "Welcome, welcome."

"Gamsahabnida," Pat says. "Thank you." Her pronunciation's perfect.

"Gamsahabnida, Mr. Choi," says Delia. As is hers.

"Please," he says. "You call me Manny or I sic my dog on you."

Audience laughter.

"Would you ladies mind if I give our viewers an idea of what happened? Why we've brought you here?"

"Not at all," Pat says.

"Okay. So Delia here goes to sleep one night after a long day of . . . you're an actress, right?"

"I was," says Delia.

"She is," says Pat.

"A long day of auditioning. In fact, you'd just booked a television show, is that correct? You go to sleep and suddenly an electrical fire starts there in your bedroom and your smoke alarm . . . which is checked . . . how often?"

"We had them checked regularly," Pat says. "Probably every three months."

"Which is probably more than most of us, right? But the alarm fails. And the fire spreads, and Delia's bed catches on fire. Now Delia's room is way upstairs and her mom and dad are downstairs, they can't smell anything yet because most of the smoke is going out the window screen. And . . ."

The camera pulls in tight on Pat, who at this point is apparently fighting off sudden tears.

Bart's a little shocked. Pat hasn't cried once over this. Not that he's seen.

"It's okay, Patricia. Can I continue?"

She nods.

"Well, what happens next is the amazing part. Caity, Delia's friend here . . ."

"Best friend," Delia quietly corrects.

"Delia's *best* friend here smells the smoke. But she's outside that night. Mom and dad are out of earshot and Caity knows she has to take action. *But.* Delia is on the second floor. So what does Caity do, Delia?"

"She climbed a tree."

"She climbs a tree! This dog, sitting right here, climbs *fifteen feet* up a tree next to Delia's window, jumps on the roof, pushes her way through the window screen, runs *through* the fire, and pulls Delia *out* of the fire which by this point has *engulfed* her bed."

In the audience, a collective murmur of astonishment.

"Mom and dad and brother . . ."

"Robbie," Delia says.

". . . Robbie get to the room just as this is happening, they *witness* this dog saving their daughter and sister's life."

Choi glances stage left, nods, smiles.

Robbie's been watching all this from the couch, mostly grinning. But he's frowning now. Bart wants to say something to him but doesn't know what.

"Okay folks," says Choi, "we'll break right here for a moment. We'll be right back after this word from our sponsors, with Delia, Patricia, and Caity Cross, ladies and gentlemen!"

"Pause it here, Bart," says Patricia.

He hits the button. Freeze-frame on Choi's big grin.

"Tell your father what happened here, Delia."

Any evidence of sleepiness is gone now. Delia is alert and he thinks, decidedly uncomfortable.

"He asked us how we were. If we needed anything. We said we were fine."

"And?" says Patricia.

"He asked Caity if she needed anything. He was kidding. Caity was watching him the whole time. I said it was okay and he said what was okay? and I said she likes you, you mean well. Which she did, because *he* did mean well, you could tell. And he said, of course I do and he just looked at me and then he asked me what was I thinking? So I told him. I told him that he could be a good person if he wanted to."

He looks from her to Pat.

"To a national TV host she says this," says Pat. "He didn't know how in hell to respond, that was clear. The director counted him down and he was still trying to figure it out when we were back up again. Play the rest."

He hits play.

"We're sitting here with our amazing . . . our amazing guests," Choi is saying, "Patricia Cross, her brave daughter, Delia, and their hero dog, Caity. Patricia, tell us about Delia's recovery process."

"It hasn't been easy, Manny. All the surgeries, the home treatments. It's our whole life right now. But our girls are getting better every day, that's the most important thing."

His wife is composed, even if Choi immediately isn't.

"It's been pretty tough on you financially, I imagine?"

"I'd be lying if I said it hasn't. But we'll get through it . . . somehow."

"Not only have you had to deal with Delia's recovery but Caity's as well, right?"

"Yes."

"Did you have pet insurance?"

"We didn't even have insurance for ourselves, no."

He settles back in his chair. "When I heard your story, I reached out to one of our sponsors, Flippy Chow, and they were so moved by Caity's bravery that they sent this, along with their very best wishes."

A curtain opens behind them stage right and two PAs wheel out an extravagant miniature firehouse, with a fireplug in front of two wide garage doors and three windows above and you can see the old-fashioned slide-pole through the middle one. Choi gets out of his chair.

"C'mon. Check it out!"

They follow him over, and it's only then that Bart realizes what the thing really is. A firehouse, yes. But also a doghouse. A doghouse just big enough for Caity. Who sniffs at it and then paws at one of the doors, which opens right up for her.

"Flippy Chow's designers built this especially for her, just for Caity!"

She sticks her head inside and emerges with a dog bone as long as Bart's forearm only thicker and gnarly, and immediately begins gnawing at it, working it between her paws. *Awwwww*s and laughter from the audience.

"One hundred percent real beef, ladies and gentlemen. Made right here in the good old USA! Our many thanks to the people at Flippy Chow. And remember, folks, your dog will *flip* for Flippy Chow! Do me a favor, Delia, and lift that fire hydrant up there."

His daughter's hesitant. But she does as he asked. The hydrant slides open on a pair of runners. Inside is a piece of scroll-type paper tied with a big fluffy red bow.

"Hey, what's this?" Choi says. "Take a look, Delia."

But instead of opening it, she passes the paper over to Pat.

It isn't what Choi wanted but he rolls with it.

"What does it say, Mrs. Cross?"

She slips off the bow. Scans it briefly. Then puts her hand to her mouth in amazement.

"A Visa Platinum card," says Choi, "from our friends at Capital One and PetSmart. Good for anything Caity needs at PetSmart. The veterinarian, great big bones, hey, anything at all. For life!"

The audience erupts into delighted applause, shouts, whistles. And Delia takes exactly that moment to bend down to Caity and start play-wrestling with her, tussling over the bone, laughing. So that her hoodie drops from her head to her shoulders. And there they are, all of them, framed in a wide shot, Pat clenching the paper in her hand, Delia and Caity seeming oblivious, off in their own world, Choi looking stricken.

The audience gasps. Then there's silence.

The camera dollies in tight on Manny, a wash of sympathy on his face and then to Delia, who for all the world might be any happy young girl playing with her dog. Except for all that scarring. Except for that.

Choi finds his voice. "Delia?"

"Mmmm?" In the tussle Caity's winning.

"Delia? Can I have you back for a moment?"

Titters from the audience. They're beginning to relax again. Delia lets go of the bone and turns her attention back to Choi.

"This brings me to our next surprise," he says. "Please welcome our next guests, Gerald Stone, president and CEO of Stone Pharmacies. And you all know the host of *Eye of the Beholder*, Dr. Lively Hamilton."

Polite applause for Stone, a thin gray man in an immaculate dark suit, and a much heavier appreciation for the glamorous celebrity doctor—mid-forties, tanning-bed brown, with wide hoop earrings and probably a dozen bracelets dangling from her left arm. Both of them smiling to beat the band.

Choi invites them to sit and waves Pat and Delia over to their own chairs. They all settle in.

"Patricia, Delia, I phoned Mr. Stone here at his office yesterday, and ten minutes after our conversation he was on his company plane to fly out here to . . . well, I'll let you explain, Gerald."

Stone clears his throat. "Thanks, Manny. Mrs. Cross, Delia, as I hope you know, we at Stone Pharmacies are committed to bringing the American people the finest quality pharmaceuticals for every need. And on behalf of my entire executive board and the thousands of employees across this great country, we've committed to covering the costs of all your medication needs for the next ten years. This includes retroactively picking up the tab for all the medicines you've had to purchase thus far without benefit of insurance. And all of us at Stone Pharmacies hope that helps, just a little."

Huge applause.

Hell, Bart wants to applaud himself. He's been expecting a very good paycheck for the show but that's all. Certainly not this. This was going to help get them off the hook big-time. Fucking amazing.

"Wow," he says. He looks to Pat, who smiles at him and nods. Even Robbie's grin's back.

"What do you think, mom?" Choi is saying. "Will that work for you?"

Pat's face is buried in her hands again. He can't tell if there are tears behind the hands or not. But her body's shaking and she uncovers her eyes and yes, damned if she isn't crying again. She wipes away the tears and reaches over for Manny and gives him a hug, then to Stone and shakes his hand clasped in both her own and mouths a silent *thank you*.

"Will that work, Delia? Is that gonna work for you?"

"Sure," she says. "Thank you, Mr. Stone."

"We're going to help, okay? Okay with you, Delia?"

She smiles and shrugs. Clearly not the huge, grateful response they're looking for. But a smile is all they get. So the camera doesn't linger.

But Choi is unconcerned. Choi is on a roll.

"Because that's not all. Dr. Hamilton?"

Hamilton leans in with her thousand-watt smile, familiar to her viewers he guesses but reading totally phony to him. He can almost smell the perfume and hear the tinkle of expensive jewelry.

"Well, Manny, when you phoned last night I was in surgery but as soon as I received your message I also committed myself right then and there to donate my services as a cosmetic surgeon to help restore Delia's lovely skin to as close to the way it was as is humanly possible, for however long it takes, with everything at my disposal."

Jesus, Bart thinks, they're just full of surprises. Why hasn't Pat told him about all this stuff right away? The bills, the surgery. It's a fucking windfall!

Onscreen Choi is practically beside himself.

"Wow! Wow! *Wowowow!* Patricia, you had to pull Delia from the hospital before all her surgeries were complete, didn't you."

"It's true. The costs were . . . too much. So once the life-saving procedures were done, we had to forgo cosmetic surgery for the time being, until I could figure out how to pay for it all . . . "

"Well, you don't have to worry about *that* anymore, do you. Does she, Doctor?"

"Not at all. Not one bit. We're going to cover absolutely everything."

Bart's guessing that the applause-meter is off the charts this time.

"What do you say, Delia? Do you want Dr. Hamilton here to help you?"

And later on he thinks, *this is why my wife didn't want to discuss the show on the telephone, why her demeanor has been so detached and strange watching it, why she's announced neither of their amazingly generous gifts to him.*

His daughter looks down at Caity, then at Manny Choi, and finally at the doctor.

"No, thank you," she says.

Roman picks up the phone and hits their number on speed dial. He thinks, I can't believe this. Pat's not going to believe this. *Nobody's* going to believe this.

Talk about your silk purse and sow's ear.

Moments like these were few and far between in his business which was mostly poring over contracts or prospective contracts, amending them and sending them out again, sometimes over and over until they got things right, all these indies now, these newbies, making the day-to-day deals which keep him and his clients afloat, none of whom are huge clients though certainly damn respectable ones, reliable working actors, actresses, and performers—and he takes pride in the fact that he *keeps* them working, dammit—fielding ridiculous offers and requests and generally acting as a buffer between them and what he sometimes laughingly refers to as the *business-world* of entertainment.

So moments like this are fucking priceless.

It was maybe four years ago now that he was rolling his carry-on through the Atlanta airport, hurrying to catch the shuttle for his connecting flight to LAX because Atlanta was a bear on scheduling. He was almost going to be late when he looked down to the high-gloss floor in front of him and there, wafting in a slight breeze, waving as though to beckon him personally amid the hundreds of people who tramped by every hour—no, every few minutes—was a one-hundred-dollar bill and a single, the single resting on top and slightly to the side.

He stooped and pocketed the both of them and caught his plane with fifteen minutes to spare.

Today feels a little like that. Stars in alignment. Lucky and easy, both. These people were total professionals. The contract would be in perfect order.

All he has to do is pass on by and pick it up.

Her phone rings twice and then she's on the line. She doesn't sound happy to hear him.

He'll fix that.

Midway through the call she has to sit down on the bed. And where were her cigarettes?

There. In the table by the flat-screen.

His phone has been ringing off the hook all morning, he says. Everybody wanting a piece of her daughter, a piece of Delia. Newspapers, magazines, another morning talk show, Fox News, feelers for a fucking supporting role in a *movie* for god's sake!

And now this.

He laughs. "You don't know what you've got here, do you, Pat. Well I do. Delia rejecting that surgery was a goddamn stroke of genius. And what did she say at the end of it? Her closing lines? *'I'm just me. This is who I am.'* Just like she did on the Latoya interview. Same thing, like a goddamn fucking *mantra*. Like she's proud of who she is, no matter what she looks like. Do you know how many kids out there have image problems? And how many parents are dealing with it?

"Lady Gaga's got this Born This Way Foundation, right? It's a fantastic success. And for a damn good reason. It addresses all the kids who feel different, ostracized, left out or left behind. Outsiders. With what she's saying, so does Delia. And she's her own most extreme example of exactly what she's talking about. Exactly what she's selling. Her own amazing poster child for the cause!

"I want you to think about this. The *Pearl* show is the number one talk show in America. Makes Manny Choi look like some *Gilligan's Island* rerun, ratings-wise. The deal's all set and all we need are the signatures on paper. We'll have contracts by tomorrow. Once she's on the air, and says what she says . . . well, Patricia, darlin', we've got our *own* foundation. We'll have every news agency in the country calling—CNN, the *New York Times*, and don't even think about the Internet, about social media—hell, this could easily go worldwide, you know what I'm saying?

"Pat? Pat? Are you there?"

She's there, all right. There and a thousand places all at once.

She is there. Arrived. Patricia Catherine Delancy Cross. With her daughter. With Delia.

THIRTEEN

There's nothing much for him to do except watch it all go down. And Robbie can't say it isn't exciting. He isn't bored. There have never been so many people in his house or outside his house for one thing, for sure never this many strangers even with the cops and firemen the night of the accident, and everybody seems to be pumped on adrenaline, not just mom and dad but all of them.

He walks out the front door and around into the garage because there's so much activity going through the pantryway. Through the open garage door he counts about thirty or more crew members outside on the street rifling through their gear and unloading the three huge trucks parked in front along with three white vans and a fancy white bus, all marked PEARL in bold blue letters along the sides and he gets out of their way as they march the stuff in.

His dad is sitting at the bar talking on his cell phone and nods to acknowledge him.

"I'm calling on behalf of our foundation," he says, "Delia's Mirror. Yes. Delia Cross. From the *Manny Choi Show*, uh-huh, that's her. We're actually unloading Pearl's crew here right now. That's right. Best platform there is. We'll be wanting to announce the charity on the show and . . ."

His mom is directing grips and electricians through the pantry hallway.

"Right through there. It gets a little tight around the end of the hall, so watch those hot points."

His mom knows the lingo.

"Roger that," says one of the grips.

He knows that the equipment costs a fortune so they're careful all right.

"I'm calling to make sure our financial structure is solid before we proceed," his dad is saying. "Taxes, licenses, all that jazz, you know? My wife and I were told you were the man to talk to. Are you the man to talk to? You are. Well, sell me then." He laughs.

It looks like dad's having a grand old time.

There's a break in the flow through the hallway so he decides to check out what's up inside. His mom leans over and gives him a kiss on the cheek along the way. *Jeez.*

In the living room he watches them, half a dozen of them, throw down wires and set up lights and reflectors without so much as a word to one another. They each seem to know exactly what the other guy is doing and why. Like they've been in his house a hundred times before and did the very same thing every time.

He likes watching them. They're working, sure, but it looks like they're having fun too working together like this as a team, seamlessly interacting. He kind of envies them. He wouldn't mind being part of a team like that someday.

He decides a Pepsi would be good so he goes back into the kitchen and snags one from the fridge.

His mom is in there now, bending over a woman seated in front of a laptop on the kitchen table along with some older guy in a ZZ

Top T-shirt. He learns later that the guy is the director, the woman, the editor.

"That's good," his mom is saying. "From the back and sides the double really does look like Delia."

"With a haze filter and a little blur you'll swear it's your daughter."

They're shooting a reenactment of the events just before the fire. Delia getting ready for bed, climbing between the sheets. The fire itself will be shot on a sound stage. They're leaving his part in it out.

He peers over his mom's shoulder. The kid does look pretty good. Same build, same height.

"Jane's a wiz at this stuff, Mrs. Cross," the director says.

"I hope so. Reenactments are usually pretty silly-looking, you know? Appreciate you guys stepping it up for us."

"Of course," he says. "Meaningful consultation."

"Throw those effects on there and give me a look. If it's as good as you say I'll sign off on it right away."

"Great. We get Pearl's approval, everything should be gravy."

His mom's back straightens at that and he can tell there's something about what he's said that's ticked her off. She doesn't say what. She turns and walks back into the garage.

He returns to the living room with his Pepsi. The guys are finished in there now and he can hear them working upstairs.

Delia sits on the floor in front of the couch with the little girl from the video, her double, dressed in exactly the same pajamas as the night of the fire, with Caity lying in front of them. The girl is petting her belly.

"Will her fur grow back?" she says.

"I don't think so," says Delia.

"That's too bad."

"She doesn't mind."

He sits down on the couch. They totally ignore him but that's no biggie. The little girl is staring at Delia's face, the scars, the stark white imprint of her hands and fingers. Good for her, he thinks, she doesn't seem bothered much at all.

"Does it hurt? The burns?"

"Sometimes."

"It's . . ."

She stops petting.

Caity looks up at her like, *hey, where'd the love go?*

"Scary?" his sister says.

"At first I thought so."

"We could tell. I mean, I could tell."

"Really? Well, now I think . . . I think it's fine."

It rings a little false. The girl is being brave.

Delia smiles. "No, you don't. But that's okay. Different is scary sometimes."

The girl looks thoughtful, then starts petting Caity again. Caity can still put on the puppy-dog eyes like a champ and she does that now. It seems to calm the girl.

"It is," she says. "Sometimes it is."

There's a comfortable silence between them. He likes seeing that.

"So. Where'd my mom go?" she says, brightening.

"If she's anything like mine, she's doing something she thinks is real, *real* important."

The girl laughs, gets up, and scampers out into the hall. Almost collides with his mom and Roman who are on their way in. And then it's as though he and Delia are a pair of ghosts, not even in the room. Because both the adults are definitely leaning toward the manic. Bearing out what Delia has just said—discussing something *real important*. Their voices hush-hush.

"Be reasonable, Pat," says Roman. "I just spent two hours on the phone with legal and they say . . ."

"I don't care what legal has to say. I told you we don't do this without *final cut!*"

"And they're giving it to you! Along with Pearl! Nobody's ever gotten that before."

"What happens if Pearl and I disagree?"

"It's mutual approval, but she has the tiebreaker . . ."

"Which means final cut!"

"They're not gonna budge, Pat. This is her show!"

"Well, then tell all these guys they can all go home, then."

She raises her chin, turns away from him, folds her arms, and stares out the window. He knows that look. It meant you're screwed. He guesses Roman does too. He pulls his phone out of his jacket pocket and stalks away, dialing as he goes.

She takes a deep breath, turns, and finally notices Delia and Caity on the floor beside her not five feet away.

"Damn, girl," she says. "Where'd you come from?"

"We've been here. Mom, have you eaten anything today?"

"No kiddo, too busy. Why don't you go get some rest. It's going to be a couple hours yet before they start shooting."

"We're not tired."

Roman leans in from the hall, still on the phone.

"Pat! I'm getting some movement. Get out here!"

Robbie and his sister exchange glances as she hurries away.

"Mom," he says.

"Mom," she says.

She scratches Caity's turned-up belly. Her front paws drift slowly up and down. If Caity were a cat, he thinks, she'd be purring.

Delia leans in close and speaks into her dog's ear.

"Mom smells funny, doesn't she. Like she's excited and scared at the same time. She smells like . . . old apples. That's it. Old apples."

Huh? he thinks.

Caity blinks up at her. Delia strokes her belly.

His sister is weird.

We're sitting on the roof and it's very best place to be right now because behind us in our room there are people rushing around one another setting things up and moving and arranging things into this corner or that corner, our things and the stuff they've brought with them, lights and boxes and whole dollies full of stuff and down on the street there's this whole big crowd of people some of them neighbors probably or just people attracted to all the activity going on and there are security guys moving the traffic along the street and one car stopped dead in front of the house honking its horn over and over like that's going to do any good, and there are cameras there and people are still unloading the trucks and vans and not a single solitary soul has spotted us sitting up here on the roof it seems, and for all this commotion behind us and below it's peaceful here in the scent of grass and trees on the breeze that ruffles our hair and glides soothing over our wounds, our hurts.

Then somebody does see us. A woman. Standing alone on the sidewalk across the street. She looks familiar but we can't place her. She's wearing a nice simple dress. She gives us a little wave. Then turns and glances back at us once and smiles as she walks away.

We're sitting on the roof and it's the very best place to be.

Pat flushes the downstairs toilet for the fourth time today and checks herself in the mirror. Her digestive system has been playing hell with her all morning and she never gets this way, not for any of Delia's shoots, not for the Choi show, never. Fuck it. She runs a brush through her hair. She looks good. So yeah, fuck it.

The AD almost trips over her as she steps out into the hall.

"We're ready to shoot up there, Mrs. Cross. If you want to have a look."

"I'll pass," she says. "I trust you guys."

I need a break, she thinks. A cigarette and a break. I need to get out of here. On her way to the patio she notices the double—Daisy her name is—and her mother climbing the stairs.

"Can Delia and Caity come to my ballet thingy?" the little girl is asking.

"A dog at the ballet. You'd love that, wouldn't you."

"She's the most polite dog I ever met."

She is that, Pat thinks, unless you're Roman. Where the hell is Roman, anyway?

He's on the patio. *Great minds,* she thinks. Only Roman's working. He's on the phone, pacing back and forth. She sits down on one of the loungers and listens.

"I hear y'all clear as a cowbell. But it ain't gonna wash with my client is all."

Roman's Okie-isms really come out when he's negotiating.

I'm just a good ol' boy.

But you'd better not mistake him for a hick.

He rolls his eyes at her. She digs out her Winstons and lights one and pulls the flask out of her pocket, unscrews the top, and takes a nice long hit. Roman, listening on the phone, waves to her to pass it over so she does. He takes a pull and hands it back.

"Well, then we'll just have to ask all these folks to go on home. No sir. That's not a threat. It's fact."

She likes how he's hard-lining them. Exactly what she wants. She takes another hit and puts the flask back in her pocket.

She hears cheering from the street. A production assistant, Kitty, pokes her head from behind the sliding glass door.

"Pearl's here," she says.

"Okay, thanks Kitty."

"I'll get back to you," Roman says. "Pearl's here."

He hangs up the phone.

"Got any Altoids?" she asks.

"Sure, darlin'. Always prepared."

He fishes around in his jacket pocket.

"I'll take three," she says.

Damned if she's not better-looking in person, Bart thinks. Big wide eyes, full lips, flawless café-mocha skin. A very young early fifties. And she's smaller. Five-two or five-three maybe. Thinner too. But she's really something.

She's like this wave of sheer *confidence* that's come crashing through his front door, walking in like she owns the joint, star power and quiet authority all the way, surrounded by these six guys in black suits and ties who looked like their last gig's been Obama at the G7 summit.

He has a sudden deeper understanding of the word *magnetism*. Because the entire room is drawn to her instantly. You can't take your eyes off her and you can't help but step a little closer, into her sphere. He guesses everybody feels it, including his family. Because he turns around and there's Patricia and Robbie standing right behind him, Delia and Caity appearing at his side.

Kitty the PA is handing her a frothy coffee in a woolly mammoth mug. She accepts and smiles warmly.

"Tell Humphry to break up that crowd out there, will you?" she says. "We want neighbors, we'll get neighbors. Not now."

"Done," says Kitty and rushes away.

"Where's the family?" she says.

Howard, the director, is right by her side. Bart hadn't even seen him arrive.

Magnetism.

"Right over here," he says.

They step forward and Howard introduces them and they shake hands. Pearl's hand is warm and smooth. She squats down to eye level for Caity. Her expression and body language tell him the woman likes dogs. This is not going to be another John Latoya. Good.

"Hey, pooch," she says and shakes her paw.

She straightens. "Okay, first of all it's Pearl. Just Pearl. We're going for informal and relaxed, right? We're all friends. They tell me our boys and girls here will have us ready in about fifteen or twenty, but Patricia? I gotta ask you a favor first."

"Of course. Anything. What do you need?"

"A powder room, sugar. My eyeballs are floatin'."

"Sure, absolutely, right this way."

He can't help but notice the sway of her hips.

Among other things, Pearl is hot.

At the bathroom doorway Pearl grasps her wrist. A firm grip.

"Talk with me a sec, mom," she says. "So many people out there, you could stir 'em with a stick."

She gives the wrist a gentle tug. Pat hesitates, confused. This is not the ladies' room at the Hyatt where they'd maybe go to share some girl thing.

"Oh, c'mon, Patricia. One of the perks of being a lady is we have a quiet office like this just 'bout anywhere we go."

She steps inside and shuts the door. Pearl pulls up her skirt and pulls down her panties and sits. Pat turns ninety degrees away and leans against the doorjamb.

"Hotter than a two-dollar pistol out there. How y'all live like this I don't know."

"You get used to it."

"I've heard that. *You get used to it.* People say the same thing about Detroit. I like the cold up there, though. I grew up in Sarasota. You want to talk about hot? August in Sarasota is one version of pure hell."

Mercifully the tinkling stops. Pearl sighs, flushes the toilet, adjusts her clothing and steps over to the sink. Squeezes out some soap and begins thoroughly washing her hands.

"So what's this I hear 'bout you telling everyone to go home?" she says.

We're having this conversation *here*? she thinks. She doesn't know what she's expected but surely not this.

"I . . . I'm very concerned with the way Delia . . . how Delia's story is presented to the public."

"As you should be, darlin'. As you should be. But this sounds like business to me, not story. My boys haven't been accommodating enough for you? That it?"

"They've been accommodating, but I don't like the final-cut clause, to be quite honest."

"I hear you. Damn contracts always make you feel like you're signin' your life away, don't they?"

"Yes, but it's not my life. It's Delia's and I'm her mother, so it's my job to protect . . ."

". . . to protect her interests. 'Course it is."

She turns off the faucets and dries her hands on the towel and the southern accent mysteriously disappears.

"The only issue I maybe have is with you, Patricia Cross. I'm wondering what kind of mother puts her injured daughter on display in front of millions of people in the first place, for money, right on the heels of a horrible experience like your little girl's been through. How long's it been? Three months? Four?"

She starts to protest, because that's totally unfair, *it is!* goddammit. But Pearl cuts her off.

"All this money we're paying you, is that all going into a trust fund for Delia?"

"I . . . there've been bills . . ."

"So the answer is no, it's not. You need to pay the gardeners to keep that yard looking top notch, you need to hit the beauty parlor, and I'm betting your electric bill on this place is impressive as hell, with all these nice high ceilings and all."

Pearl's eyes narrow. She takes one step toward her and the spacious bathroom suddenly feels like she's standing in a closet, her back to the wall. This lady's *scary.*

"You're trying to shake me down, aren't you," she says.

"I'm not . . ."

"Of course you are. Here's how it is. You get no final cut. That's mine. And you're not nearly big enough to rate an exception. You get no bump in the money 'to compensate' either. You want to walk? You go ahead. Walk. I can spread these expenses on my fucking toast tomorrow morning. And if you do walk, here's what you get. An instant rep as the hopped-up stage mom who was stupid enough to let Pearl slip right through her fingers."

She turns to check her makeup in the mirror.

"Don't get me wrong. Your daughter and her sweet ol' dog are about the most precious thing I've seen all year and her story is going to inspire and maybe even help a helluva lot of people because helping people and giving them hope in a shit-ass world full of money-grubbing, power-tripping no-talent leeches like you is what I do. So I'm going to get her story out there. Despite your sorry ass. You following me on this? We clear?"

When she faces Pat again her eyes are softer and the southern lilt is back.

"Oh, lookit you. Squirmin' like a worm on an anthill. Relax, girl. It ain't gotta be this way, Patricia! Can you trust me to cut the show to your likin'?"

She feels like she's been hit by a hammer—no, mugged in an alley by six teenage boys and they're finally letting her up again.

"Y-yes, ma'am . . . ," she says.

"Well, see there? Problem solved. Alright . . ."

She glances at her watch.

"You get your boy to sign off on that piece o' paper and the two of us can get out there and make hay while the sun shines. You ready? Good."

She moves on past her and out the door.

Roman has ringside for this one, seated next to Bart, Delia, and Robbie in front of the monitor in the hall where he can see Pearl and Patricia together by the table in the living room.

Not ten minutes ago they'd been in the kitchen, finally signing contracts. Pat had given him no explanation as to why final cut was no longer an issue and he hadn't asked. The deal was going through. The shoot was going forward. She signed and Pearl signed and he signed and that was all that mattered. They'd talk later.

Cameras are rolling. Pat and Pearl sit across from one another on the couch. Between them, on the coffee table, crackers and cheese, muffins and a carafe of lemonade. All very homey. The director points to Pearl and she leans in to address her audience, ever the gracious southern hostess.

"I'm here with Patricia Cross, talkin' about the sensation caused by her eleven-year-old daughter Delia on Manny Choi's show last week. A sensation that's sparked a national debate 'bout the importance of self-image among children and young teens. Welcome, Patricia."

"Thank you, Pearl." She looks nervous, he thinks.

He'd wondered aloud this morning why Bart wasn't invited in on this particular shoot, it was such an important one. *I get jittery in front of a camera*, Bart said. *I stammer. I get this ridiculous expression on my face.* Pat had vigorously confirmed this. So be it.

But now she's the one looking nervous. Not like the Patricia he saw on the Choi show or any of the previous interviews. Glancing sideways or down into her lap. *Don't blow it, Patricia,* he thinks. *Pretty please.*

"Now the camera doesn't lie," Pearl says. "And when I watch this Choi clip very closely—watch *you* very closely—you want to know what I see?"

Pat tenses. He can feel it from here.

My god, she's *scared,* he thinks. She's actually scared. She's smiling but . . .

"I see shock," Pearl says. "I see a woman caught completely off guard. Unprepared. What Delia said on the air wasn't planned, was it."

"N-no. Not at all."

"So when Delia flat-out *rejects* the offer of free cosmetic surgery, tell us what's going through your mind, Patricia?"

Better now, he thinks. A bit better. Pearl is leaning in close, giving the impression that hey, they're just a pair of girlfriends having a good ol' down-home chat. It's a talent she has and it's working on her guest.

For a moment there Pat had him worried, had looked like she felt she was under attack.

"Well, it was a shock at first. I mean, since the beginning of all this, Delia's handled everything in such an amazing way, she's been so levelheaded, so strong. So at first I couldn't fathom why she'd reject it. It was so very, very kind of Manny and Dr. Hamilton to make the offer. And I was sort of embarrassed, I guess . . ."

"Wait. Hold right there for a sec. Now this seems important to me. You were *embarrassed,* Patricia?"

"Because Delia didn't . . . wasn't playing along . . ."

"Playing along."

Flat. Like an accusation. Pat bites at her lower lip. He can see beads of sweat forming at her temples.

What the fuck is Pearl doing here?

"Well, yes. I mean, someone makes a generous offer in that sort of situation, you kind of have to . . ."

"Have to?"

"Yes, well, go with it. Say yes! Of course! Thank you! I mean, there are all these people watching. So I didn't know what to do. Maybe I should have anticipated somehow . . ."

She's clearly flustered. He glances over at the family sitting beside him. They're riveted. Delia's brow is furrowed with concern, as is Bart's.

Pearl reaches over and gives Pat's leg a squeeze.

This was all about drama, he realizes. She was simply going for drama.

"Oh, no no no, girl. I'm not judgin' you. I think that's the same reaction any one of us could have had. Go on."

The touch seems to help immensely.

How does she *do* that? Roman wonders.

Pat takes a deep breath.

"Well, it's clear to me now that Delia's reaction was correct. There is *nothing* she needs to change about herself. I mean, we all have scars, don't we? And what I've come to realize is that if Delia has that much confidence in herself, in her own self-image, then why couldn't we put together a way for her to get out there and share that confidence with other kids. And even adults."

Pearl smiles into the camera. "Our brave veterans, anyone?"

"Yes. Yes, exactly. I think what Delia was trying to say is that if she's okay with herself and her scars, everyone else out there could be too. Our scars are what build our character, aren't they? But a lot of people . . . I guess they didn't understand. It obviously hit some of them, some of the viewers, really hard that Delia would turn down the chance to look . . ."

"She turned down the chance to look *normal* again, right?"

"Yes. And I guess I'm a little ashamed for . . . for not accepting the way she . . . for not backing her up right away."

And there's Pearl's hand again, giving Pat's leg a motherly pat. Patricia nods and bows her head, takes the hand, and squeezes it. Pat is acting now. This is not genuine. To him that's obvious. It wouldn't be to most everyone. The camera's reading it just fine. But he wonders how Delia's taking it.

"You've got nothing to be ashamed of, pretty lady," Pearl says. "We're here to talk this out. All of it. Now there were a lot of mothers out there who were absolutely furious with you over this, weren't there."

"Quite a few."

Pearl shuffles some papers on her lap. Correspondence? Notes? Or just props?

"That you wouldn't insist on the surgery."

"Yes."

"I've got some *words* for these mothers here in a minute."

Pat can't seem to help but grin a little.

"After the break, we're going to bring Delia out here so y'all can hear her for yourself. And you do not want to miss that. Thank you, Patricia. Folks, you stay where you are, we'll be right back."

She holds for a beat.

"Cut. Okay. Great. Let's reset. Patricia? Excellent, darlin'. You're a natural, aren't you? Wanna come take a gander at the tape we're gonna run before the next segment?"

"Sure, Pearl."

"Roman? Family? You're all invited."

He gets up, as do Bart and Robbie. Delia stays where she is, petting Caity.

"You okay, Deal?" he says.

"We're fine," she says. "We might go outside for a while."

"You go right on ahead. Say hello to the real world for me."

"Okay," she says.

Delia, he thinks, is a very literal-minded young girl.

There's this scratching sound. *Skritch, skritch, skritch.* Like nails on a blackboard. No. Like nails on a door.

It's coming from outside. She and Caity are sitting on the staircase. So how can it be coming from *outside*? But Delia's sure. It is.

Her mom and dad, Robbie, Roman, and Pearl are all crowded around the dining room table, watching the editor, seated, pull up a video file from her hard drive—some "man on the street" interviews. She isn't interested. She and Caity have fallen behind and they haven't missed them. They get up off the stairs and walk right past them, unnoticed, to the sliding glass doors.

Behind her she hears some woman going on and on, her voice tinny on the monitor.

". . . you ask me, it's just not right. That girl is just a young girl, she doesn't know what's best for her. It's her mother's responsibility to . . ."

Over that Delia can hear the scratching.

She opens the doors and they step outside.

Into a kind of magic.

When she was little her favorite book was one her parents had actually bought for Robbie because it was a boy's book they said, and the main character was a little boy. But she never thought of *Where the Wild Things Are* as a boy's book or a girl's book, it was just an adventure into a dreamworld on a little boat that took you to someplace inhabited by monsters. Big, bug-eyed, goofy monsters drawn so sharply that they seemed to jump right out of the page at you, crystal clear, in all that carefully drawn pen and ink detail. The colors were impossibly bright, like the sun was shining just for them and the little boy joining them off the boat.

Her *lawn* is like that now. Her own familiar backyard. Like her vision has become suddenly sharper. The tables and chairs on the patio, the flagstones beneath them, each leaf on the trees, each dandelion and blade of grass standing out in knife-edge clarity from one another, outlined as though in vivid black ink. The production assistant Kitty is outside smoking a cigarette. She can see every wrinkle in her jeans and T-shirt. Her face and forearms sparkle with sunlight. The smoke from her cigarette forms a distinct solemn trail into the still, warm air.

But what draws her is the back fence. And in front of that, the swing set and slide. They blaze stark with light.

Skritch. Skritch.

The sounds are coming from over there.

Caity leads the way.

"Can I get you ladies anything?" Kitty says as they pass. She stuffs her crew sheet into her back pocket and snuffs out her cigarette on the lawn. Bends to police her butt.

It takes Delia a moment to respond, distracted by the shimmering glint in Kitty's pale blue eyes.

"Doggy bathroom break," she says.

Kitty laughs. "Okay," she says and turns to go inside.

Climb the slide, she hears herself say. *You got to climb to see.*

So she does. Climbs the ladder while Caity takes a running leap and bounds up the slippery slide. They meet up top and sit.

And it's like she's in that little boy's boat, in the crow's nest. She can see all around.

"What do you think, Caits?" She strokes her dog's broad gleaming back. "Almost like the roof, isn't it? This is us. This is where we live."

Caity's eyes blink at her once and then hold steady on her own.

Skritch.

She *sees* them before she sees them.

There in Caity's brimming eyes.

"You *play* with them, don't you!" she says. "I saw you. Caits! You were *playing* with them!"

She looks down below. Directly to the fence. To the pair of gray kits, young foxes rolling and wrestling with each other in the dirt and scratching at the corner fence post. Stopping to gaze up at them, a pair of potential playmates not so far away and wrestling some more. Tiny creatures filled with the sheer fun of living. Their monsters. Their wild things.

"Oh, Caits," she says. "If you want to jump this damn old fence and run away I'd understand. I honestly, really would. There's a whole world out there, isn't there."

But Caity's Caity, and she's going nowhere without her. Delia hugs her tight.

When she hears the silence below and looks down again the kits have vanished.

Pat has the distinct impression that her daughter isn't taking this sufficiently seriously.

"Delia! Get down from there. Makeup!"

What the hell are she and the dog doing up the freakin' slide, anyway?

"I don't do makeup, remember?"

"You know what I mean. Get down."

She moves like molasses but she climbs on down the ladder. Caity takes the express route.

In the living room the cameras have been reset and they're ready to go. The director seats Delia next to her, hood turned down, burn scars there for all the world to see. Caity isn't in this segment but sits off-camera next to the sound mixer. Fine with Pat.

This isn't about some hero dog anymore. This is about the burning.

In the follow-up to the street interviews Pearl asks her about the negative responses and Pat tells her she understands where some of these parents are coming from but that they're wrong, her daughter knows her own mind to an amazing degree, and that she's convinced Pat that yes, she's totally ready to face the world as is.

So now it's Delia's turn.

"You've had a lot of press over the past couple of weeks, Delia, and we've talked to your mom and know what her thoughts are, but what about you? How is Delia taking all this?"

"I'm fine."

"Not overwhelmed by all the attention?"

"Nope."

Short answers. The interviewer's nightmare, thinks Pat. *Again.*

"So after some reflection, do you still feel good about rejecting that offer for cosmetic surgery?"

"I don't think about it much anymore."

"You don't?"

If anybody knows how to crack a nut, she thinks, Pearl does.

"Okay. So what *is* on your mind these days?"

"Us, I guess. Mom and dad. Robbie. Caity."

"Family. That's the most important thing, isn't it. But sweetie, don't you ever think about the way you look? The way others might view you?"

"Why would I?"

If this is pissing Pearl off she isn't showing it.

"Well, most people are very, very concerned about the way they appear to others. I guess that's one reason we wanted to meet you. You have a very special outlook on life. One that your mom thinks you should share with a lot of folks out there, who may not be as self-assured as you are."

Delia seems to consider this.

"To tell the truth, I don't get it," she says. "Why me? Why should I? Isn't that what you do? Reassure people? Isn't that your job?"

"Well, yes. In a way, I suppose. But I'm not . . ."

"Real?"

Pat can't stop herself. "Delia!"

It pulls Pearl up short too. For a second. For a second it's pin-drop quiet. Then she laughs.

"It's okay, mom. Girl, I'm afraid I'm 'bout as real as it gets! Just ask my director."

"You know what I mean, Pearl. You're an actor. Like I was."

She doesn't know which is more shocking—what she's said or using Pearl's first name, that grown-up intimacy. She realizes that right now, at right this moment, she barely knows this girl, her own daughter.

"Truthfully? I can't act my way out of a paper bag, hon. But you, I've seen your work. And you were just about the most adorable thing . . ."

"Were, yes. Past tense. Thank you."

"Are, little sister! Still are."

"Really? Think I'll be good for your ratings? Sell a lot of drugs for you?"

There is no way to know what the camera's catching but Pat can feel the anger in Pearl settling in deep and she knows from recent experience that she's perfectly capable of showing it.

But she can bury it too.

"Sell drugs. What do you mean, Delia?"

"That's what your show does, right? You talk a while about, I don't know, cooking or shoes or somebody's divorce or that woman whose baby got its fingers eaten off by the family's pet ferret—I saw that one—and then you go to a commercial for Zaebocam or Hannaxim and then you talk some more. Right?"

This is so far off point she can't believe she's hearing it. She almost opens her mouth again but Pearl gets there first.

"That's an excellent observation, Delia. Talking's what I do. But I don't sell drugs. That's our advertisers. They buy ad space from us and . . ."

"I know. I did lots of commercials."

"And I understand you'll be doing them again. This time for a very worthy cause. Your charity. Delia's Mirror."

Delia laughs. No. *She giggles.*

"My charity," she says.

And Pat realizes this is never going to make it to the finished cut, never. She has to wonder how much of the rest of it will either. She is suddenly furious with Delia. Sick to death of her surprises, sick of her selfish games. Why the hell can't she just stick to the fucking program like everybody else does? Who does she think she is?

"It is *your* charity, isn't it?" Pearl's voice is dry as sandpaper. The question is to Delia but she feels like it's aimed at her.

Whose charity is this?

"Maybe we could take a break?" Pat offers.

Which is when Caity leaps into the shot. Straight to Delia's feet.

"Whoa! Hold your biscuits. Here we go!" Pearl says. "A surprise guest! This is Caity! How you doin', girl?"

Caity just pants, tongue lolling and tail wagging, blinking at her.

Pearl seems okay with the distraction but Pat isn't.

"Deal, it's not quite time for Caity yet," she says. "Tell her to go lay down."

She reaches over and squeezes her daughter's shoulder. Maybe just a little harder than she intended. Delia flinches. Caity's tail stops wagging. She looks slowly from Pearl over to Pat. Lowers her head.

She removes her hand from Delia's shoulder.

"A little time to regroup, Pearl?" she says. "Do you mind?"

"In a sec, doll. I want to see if Caity here can shake. Can you give me a shake, Caiters?"

"She likes it when you call her wiggle-butt," says Delia.

"Wiggle-butt? Hey, wiggle-butt. Can you give me a shake?"

Caity trots over, butt going. Sits down and gives Pearl's outstretched hand a lick.

"*Eeeuuuwwww*, dog lips! Good girl! Just like my Soozie. Now how 'bout that shake?"

Caity raises a paw and complies and Pearl ruffles the fur on her head. Delia's smiling, watching closely. Pat feels strangely left out of it, thrust out of the circle, ignored. It grates at her. None of this is going remotely the way she wants.

"Okay," Pearl says. "Let's take that break. Howard?"

The cameras cut. The lights dim. Everybody seems to relax but her. There's no way she can relax. This is a mess. Delia is making a total mess of it, dammit.

She gets out of her chair and stalks alone into the kitchen.

His wife is crying and these aren't stage tears, these are the real thing and Bart can feel the anger and frustration that's causing them—hell, he's feeling his share of frustration too—but right now she's the one going back onstage, not him, and he and Roman are there to console her, that's their job right now so they listen and try to reassure her but she isn't having any of it, she's pissed to the max and she's saying, *I just want to get this fucking thing over with* when Pearl appears behind them and pulls her aside and Pearl is not happy either.

All they could do is watch. Pearl's eyes narrow down to slits.

"Look, hon," she says, "we're in this now so yes, let's get this fucking thing over with. But you get your shit together and do it like a *professional*, do you hear me? You don't interrupt. You don't make faces. You don't . . ."

Roman raises a hand to stop her.

"Now hold on just a minute, Pearl," he says.

She doesn't even spare him a look.

"And if your swamp leech here raises a hand to me again he's gonna pull back a bloody stump, understand?"

Jesus! He's glad it's Roman on the receiving end and not him. But even he feels humiliated. He can't imagine how the agent's feeling. *Swamp leech?* But Roman just seems to suck it up. Like she's said nothing of any consequence at all.

His wife has gone all stoic too.

"Everything's fine," she says. "I just needed a breather."

"Whatever blows your dress up, honey. You be ready in five, now."

She turns and walks away and there's Delia standing with Caity at the entrance to the kitchen so she stops and they're talking and he has to wonder how the hell *that's* going to go.

"Christ on a tricycle," Pearl says. "You're who I'm lookin' for next and there you are waitin' on me."

"We're gonna go play outside."

"We're starting back up here in five, kiddo. Hang tight."

"We're going outside for a bit."

Pearl takes a deep breath and leans down. She can smell the mints on her breath.

"Hey, little girl," she says. "I can see exactly what's going on here. This is all a bunch of nonsense to you, isn't it? Did anyone even ask you if *you* wanted all my razzmatazz in your house?"

"Nobody asked me. They told me. That's the way it always is. Even before . . ."

"Sometimes people even have a way of asking that sounds a lot like telling, huh?"

"Sometimes."

She looks steadily into Pearl's eyes. Maybe this lady has a clue, she thinks. Maybe. She likes dogs, anyway. We know that. But it doesn't pay to automatically trust strangers.

"We're not going to be friends," she tells her.

"Ouch! Roger that. And we don't have to be, darlin'. Won't hurt if it looks that way, though, right? Can we be friends in front of the camera, starting about now?"

"Will it make you all go home faster if I do?"

"You bet it will. It'll make me happier than a pig in sunshine."

She has to laugh. "I can do that," she says.

"Shake on it?"

So they do.

We're sitting on the roof under the evening stars. Our ears adjust. We're listening.

They're sitting at the kitchen table—mom, dad, Roman—all except for Robbie, who's lying on the couch reading X-Men: Fall of the Mutants *but Robbie's listening too. The pages rarely turn.*

"Pearl gets twenty-five percent ownership of the copyright as silent partner," Roman says, "but the promotion from the show alone is worth more than that."

"Then there's your fifteen percent," mom says.

"Well sure, I'm brokering the whole thing . . ."

"You didn't broker shit. Pearl just told you how it's going to be."

They're talking about a book. Our book.

"I'm on your side, Patricia."

"Yeah, go easy, hon," says dad.

"She's a goddamn bully."

"The interview went fine after the break. She seems pretty straight up to me," he says.

"She's straight up, all right. Thank you, Bart. We'll take that under advisement."

"Be nice. Have another drink."

We hear the sliding chair. Pouring. Ice. Chair.

"I love it that we're selling something that doesn't exist," says dad.

"The show doesn't run for another three weeks," says Roman. "Pearl's got a ghost writer who can have it done in two."

"A whole book?"

"Sure. Doesn't have to be Game of Thrones. *A few pictures, large typeface. Easy-breezy."*

Sliding chair. Bart's heavy footsteps. Pouring. Ice.

Sliding chair. Mom's.

"I've got to do Delia's meds and cream," she says. "Don't make any important decisions without me, okay?"

Robbie in the doorway.

"I'll do 'em," he says.

"What?"

"Delia's stuff. You guys can keep . . . doing whatever you're doing."

"Okay. Sure. Thanks, Robbie."

"No problem."

Robbie on the stairs. Robbie in the hallway. Robbie in our room. Leaning out our bedroom window.

"Hey, Deal. Time to do your creams and stuff."

We look out at the stars. We hate to leave the stars.

"Guys?"

We get up. "Sure. Okay."

Robbie unscrews the cap on the jar of skin cream and dips his fingers in. She tugs down her pajama top, baring her neck and shoulders. Beside them on the night table over a dozen bottles of pills and vitamins are arrayed according to whatever time of day or night they're to be administered. By now he knows them all.

He rubs the cream into the back of her neck. Feels the smooth uneven ribbing of scar tissue beneath his fingers.

"You tired?"

"I dunno. A little."

"Sounds like you're writing a book."

"And Pearl gets twenty-five percent. I heard."

It takes a moment to sink in. She *heard*?

"You suppose I get to read what I say before I say it?"

He laughs. "Good question."

"Boy, am I ever not sure about this."

"Don't blame you. Not your idea."

"Nope. No way."

"Second thoughts, huh?"

"*Dozens* of them! I mean, magazines, newspapers, the shows. And now . . . a book?"

He dips his fingers again and works her right shoulder.

"Ooh. *Cold.*"

"They're still goin' at it down there," he says.

"I know."

"So. What did Aunt Ev have to say?"

She'd called a little after dinnertime. He'd picked up and they talked about nothing much in particular for a minute or two and then she asked to speak to Delia. Not his mom, which he thought peculiar. But Delia.

"She'd seen me on the *Manny Choi Show*. She said he was silly."

"He was. He is."

"She said she was proud of me. She said she was never brave when she was a kid. She said she hid inside her books. Do you think I'm brave, Robbie?"

"I dunno. You're my sister. You're just Delia."

"That's what I figure."

He rubs a little harder on the left side and she winces.

"Sorry. It still hurts pretty bad, huh?"

"Yeah, but it's okay."

It isn't okay but he lets it slide.

He works in silence after that. When he's done he recaps the bottle and goes to the bathroom to get her a glass of water and then hands her the pills one by one and watches her swallow.

"Thanks, brother," she says.

"Sure. Anytime."

He stoops to pet Caity on the bed beside her and then heads toward the door.

"Thanks for carrying Caity out of the hospital," she says. "And for taking care of her in the car and all."

"Sure," he says again. "'Night Deal, 'night Caits."

He's halfway down the stairs before it occurs to him to wonder exactly how his sister knows it was him and not his dad who'd carried Caity to the car that day. As far as he knows nobody's told her.

FOURTEEN

She steps into morning sunlight and even with the dark glasses the sun blares at her like the horn section of some fucking high school marching band. The headache is killer, a hangover that two Ambien and an oxycodone have yet to dissipate.

She's sleep-deprived as hell. She'd gotten two, maybe three hours before the alarm went off and about two more once she'd batted it into submission. She wishes now that she hadn't taken those last two hours because now she's running ridiculously late but she'd given it no thought at the time, her only thought was sleep.

What was Bart thinking, trying to crawl all over her last night? It had been weeks, even a month since last she'd let him. So why now? Why last night? When it's Barnes & Noble this morning, Delia's first big signing. Sure, they'd had a few drinks over reruns of *Law & Order: Criminal Intent* but they were hardly drunk by bedtime and *Law & Order* was hardly erotica.

And if he *hadn't* tried, if he hadn't thrown his growing bulk and spreading butt on top of her, she wouldn't have gotten the hell out of bed for those two last stiff vodka martinis and her head wouldn't be splitting this morning and she wouldn't be feeling like some goddamn marionette fumbling with her purse, the cart with her suitcase and makeup kit, and the outfits for her and Delia going out to the car.

When she'd finished the drinks and went back to bed it was empty. She'd known where he was. On the couch for the night. Pouting. Typical Bart behavior. She'd probably walked right past him. Then this morning when she gets up she hears his car pulling out of the driveway, he and Robbie already gone, "*getting an early start,*" he'd say. Mr. Passive-aggressive. Damn him. He hadn't bothered to wake her, no. And that was typical Bart too. Make her squirm in order to get her shit together. Hers and Delia's.

And where the hell is Delia?

What do they do at a signing if the signer's late?

She checks her watch. They're already late—five minutes late. And even with no traffic the store is twenty-five minutes away.

Her head's pounding.

She tosses her purse into the front seat and manages to find the right key on her key ring and pops the trunk and dumps the cart inside and she's lying the clothes neatly on top of it when the front door opens and there they are, standing together, Delia and Caity.

Finally.

"C'mon, kiddo. Dad and Robbie are there already. We gotta go. We're late."

"I'm done, mom," she says.

Her hand freezes on the hood of the trunk.

"What are you talking about?" her mother says. "Get in the car."

"Mom. I'm done."

She's thought it over and over again, all last night and all this morning. There are places she just can't go. It was one thing to do the interviews, even to be interviewed on TV—and when they were talking about Caity and what Caity had done for her it wasn't bad at all, it was worth doing. It was probably even worth doing the Choi and Pearl shows, letting people know how she felt about herself. She figured that couldn't hurt.

It was honest. It was her.

But this book.

She's read this book. It's supposed to be in her voice. But it isn't. It isn't honest and it isn't her. It's a lot of self-help nonsense illustrated by examples of events she's never even heard of much less ever thought or talked about. Research, they called it. Well, it isn't her research. She thinks *Delia's Mirror* deserves its mediocre-at-best reviews and doesn't deserve its good sales at all.

The book made her want to crawl into a hole and die. Certainly not sign the thing. Not meet all these people who'd read it or were buying it in order to read it, thinking it would help somehow, thinking it was worth something. The book made her feel ashamed. Nothing in all of this has made her feel ashamed but this. So she's finished.

"No bookstore, mom. No foundation. I'm done," she says. "It's got to be about us from now on. All the rest of this stuff? I want to put it away."

"Don't be ridiculous. Get in the car."

"It's about *us*, mom. You, me, Robbie, dad, Caity. We're supposed to be a family. We're supposed to care for each other."

Her mother hasn't moved. Delia does, along with Caity. She needs to feel closer. She steps over to the car.

"Of course we care for god's sake," mom says. She's annoyed. "Why do you think we're doing this? You think I'd keep all this afloat if I didn't care about us? You've been swallowing Pearl's bullshit. You think *she* cares about us?"

"No, she probably doesn't. I know that. I'm not stupid."

"Well then stop talking stupid. Get in the car. I don't have time for this shit this morning, kiddo. Really."

She smells like fear, Delia thinks. *My mom smells like fear.*

It could practically break her heart.

She holds out her arms, moves to embrace her, Caity right there by her side.

"We need to be a family, mom, not some show, we need to forget about the book, the foundation, get rid of this thing with Roman . . ."

"What? *What did you say? What are you talking about?*"

Her mother backs away.

"It's okay, mom."

"Delia Ann Cross. What do you mean by that?"

"I know about . . . about Roman. Don't worry, I'm not gonna tell. *I love you*, mom. Caity and me, we're just not doing this stuff anymore. We just want you guys . . ."

She leans over and wraps her arms around her and immediately knows it's a mistake, she can see it, feel it an instant before it happens, before her mother screams *goddammit, you little shit!* and pushes her, pushes her hard and there's the yawning trunk of the car behind her at just the very corner of her vision as she falls and the lip of the trunk rising fast to meet her and the sound of Caity barking, one loud yip as though in pain and the sound of her neck cracking gunshot against the lip and . . .

. . . Caity is alone, gone suddenly blind, stumbling where she stands and then pulling herself up, still blind, tripping over a warm inert body and then into a second body, a pair of legs standing there belonging to someone who's screaming and kicking her away as she herself is howling wanting somehow to climb, to get in, to get out, *Caity trapped there in the dark of a sunlit day as a fog slowly rises somewhere in front of her, her hackles bristling, trails of fog drifting slowly toward her and then fast, faster, much faster, until it flickers and disappears and she can feel it deep within, a warmth, a quiet, and her vision clears and on the ground in front of her Patricia is breathing, sobbing, into the open mouth of a dead dry husk that once was a girl whose name was Delia.*

PART THREE

FIFTEEN

His mind keeps shooting blanks at him, deafening explosions that seem to have no object, no target, no sense, no direct hits. Through it all, from his father's face gone bloodless as he listened on the cell phone to dashing out of the bookstore to the race back home, his father talking, groaning, the car pulling up half on the sidewalk and half on the street and the two of them piling through the open front door to his mother on the couch wrapped in an EMS blanket with a cop, a new cop, unfamiliar to him, a balding cop in shirtsleeves and tie sitting across from her, leaning in, writing in his notepad, through all of this only bursts of understanding which first slam home and then go utterly silent inside him moment to moment.

Delia. An accident. A real accident this time. And Delia . . . dead?

No.

". . . we were racing to get out the door . . ."

His mother's hands like leaves swirling in a strong wind.

His father, beside her on the couch, reaching over, taking one of them.

". . . and Caity . . . I dunno . . . Caity was hyper this morning. Did you notice? That Caity was hyper this morning? Did you notice that?"

He has no idea what she's talking about. He can't even remember seeing Caity this morning. His father seems not to get it either. His father seems to study her, expectant, like he's been waiting for his cue, his line, but then almost misses it when it comes.

"I didn't, no."

He is talking to the cop, not to her.

"But then I've seen her get like that. Especially when . . . when Delia's upset. Those two are joined at the hip."

It hangs in the air. The cop nods. His dad has used the present tense. *Are.* But there isn't any *is* or *are* anymore, is there?

His mother lights a cigarette. The veins in her hands shift like thick blue worms burrowed shallow inside her skin.

"We were fumbling with all our stuff . . . trying to get out the door, get it in the trunk . . . and Caity . . . she just jumped right between us . . . she was too excited or something . . . and she hit Delia in the chest and her feet came out from under her and she fell and hit the car, the trunk of the car and I could hear it and I tried to wake her, to get her to breathe, you know? And Caity . . . Caity just sat there, she didn't mean it, she knew something was wrong, she just . . ."

His mother begins to cry. His father takes her in his arms, stares over the top of her head as at something distant, as though at something far away. The cop watches them, silent, his eyes soft, his face benign. Robbie looks at Caity lying at the foot of his chair. Caity is watching them too. And it's only then, looking down at Caity inches from his feet, so close he can almost feel the heat of her body beside him, hear the breath travel through her lungs, that he feels finally an access to his own feeling, his own immense unforgiveable loss, and he too begins to cry, and he sets his hand gently down to rest on her back, for solace, for the familiar, for the solid truth of her undeniably there and not forever beyond his reach.

When she is through listening and he is calm at last she moves out from beneath the warmth of Robbie's hand and slowly climbs the stairs. Everything hurts. Not just the sharp biting pain in her ribs where Patricia has kicked her but her shoulders, head and neck, an ache that travels down through her legs as she ascends and hoists herself onto the landing and into Delia's room.

A pair of socks on the floor. A towel from this morning. She smells the bed. Gathering herself against the pain she jumps up to Delia's side of the bed, to the still fresh scent of her and settles in. She can hear the voices below but the voices mean nothing to her now. She must sleep.

When she wakes the house is dark and silent but for the quiet muffled sobbing coming from Robbie's room. She can picture him clearly. Lying curled up on his side, legs pulled up nearly to his chin, the pillow pressed over his head. She could go to him but she aches. It is all she can do to shift positions on the bed. Her ribs stab her as she breathes.

She will see to him in the morning. He will be there. Now she needs to sleep. Again she settles in.

It is a quiet, private funeral. Very private. Her sister Evvie had wanted to fly out but Pat said no. Just us. And Roman. Not her mother, not her sister. On the phone Evvie had sounded terribly disappointed and Bart felt bad for her. But Pat was adamant. It surprised him that she wanted it that way. But in sum it was all to the good. No complications.

But now here they are, plenty of complications, right at his doorstep. The press. Hyenas biting at his flanks as he, Pat, Robbie, and Roman exit the SUV.

This one immediately in his face.

"Mr. Cross. Mr. Cross? What happens now?"

He brushes past the guy only to be confronted by another. *No comment* from Pat. *No comment* from Roman. Robbie with his head down as though in a rainstorm. All of them pushing through toward the front door.

"Mr. and Mrs. Cross! What are you going to do now? So sorry for your loss. What are your plans?"

Flashbulbs, video cameras, phone cameras. The works.

"Mr. Cross!"

Bite your tongue, he thinks. Play nice. *Try*, at least. Patricia's key is in the door.

"Listen, listen up!" he says. "Not that it's any of your business, guys, but we're going to take it one day at a time, okay? Okay? Now please, give us some privacy. Have a little decency."

Then they're inside. Caity at the door. He slams it shut behind him. "Jesus!"

Pat tosses her black handbag on the couch.

"'*We're gonna take it one day at a time.*' Where did you come up with that one, Bart?"

"Well hell, one of us had to say *something.*"

"Oh we did, huh? You're a fucking idiot. Hey, you could have told them that. 'I'm a fucking idiot, what do I know?' There's a real sound bite for you!"

"Look, this is hard on all of us, Pat. Have a little . . ."

"*Decency*, Bart? Was that what you were going to say? Another good one. Yes! Also brilliant!"

What the hell is her problem all of a sudden? He didn't see this nastiness at the funeral. He's very aware of Robbie, who's pegged his coat in the hall and has turned away toward the kitchen, loosening his tie. Robbie doesn't need to hear this.

"She's right, brother," says Roman. "Those shitheel trash collectors can take every scrap of footage, every word you say and turn it into anything they want. Better to just keep your mouth shut. Period."

And man, does that burn his ass. Bad enough his wife. But *Roman*? Roman all pious, crossing himself at the service. Roman at his wife's elbow through the entire thing. Roman the wised-up know-it-all hotshot agent who got them all into this goddamn mess in the first place. His son is out of earshot now. Good. He moves in.

"You know what, you dumb fucking Okie? Guess what. You've opened *your* mouth one too many times when it comes to me and my family."

Weren't expecting that, were you Roman?

"Hey, pardner. Let's just relax and have a drink. Okay?"

"No, *pardner. I'm* going to have a drink with my wife and you're going to walk your ass out the door, right now. I've had it. Your opinions are not welcome here. Go have a drink with the boys out there in the press corps, since you know them so damn well."

It's nice, *real* nice to see him back off so fast.

"Fine. Okay. That's just fine. I'll give you a call in a day or so. You need your time."

"No. You're not calling anyone. You're fired, Roman. I am not gonna have some *employee* undermine me in front of my family. Got that? *Fired.*"

"Bart . . . ," says Patricia.

"Sorry, hon. But I'm done with this prick."

He feels himself waver a little under her steady gaze. Hold firm, he thinks. Firm. That's right.

"That's just the way it's gotta be. It's all over anyway, right? Isn't it? We don't even need your services anymore. I sure don't."

And what flickers between them then? It's there and gone.

"There's a lot I could say right now, but I won't," Roman says. "I'm sorry for your loss, Bart, Patricia."

"Just go. We're done here."

He turns toward the door and stops.

"You sign off on this thing, Pat? Nothing you have to say?"

She crosses her arms, regarding him.

"My husband thinks it's best if you leave, Roman. I suggest you do."

Then he's out the door and into the crowd. Bart closes the door behind him. He feels a little sheepish now, like he probably overreacted but what the hell, sometimes you had to, didn't you? Didn't you?

"Sorry, babe," he says, "but I think this is for the best."

She gives it a beat. He can see the mind working. He knows her so well.

"Did I contradict you?" she says. "You're right. We're done with him. So. Who wants a drink?"

"Robbie, Robert . . . son . . . c'mere . . ."

He's seen his mom high before god knows, but this is something else. This is deeply, seriously, word-slurring, weavingly drunk. And from the way he's sitting slouched in front of her at the dining room table, his father isn't much better.

All he wants to do is sit with his Pepsi in front of the TV for an hour or so before he has to go up to do his dumb homework, sit next to his sad-looking, depressed-looking dog on the couch with nothing on his brain but some cop show or something but his mother's calling him over.

"Pull up a chair. Something I want to say to you."

The television beckons. He can hear a Pringles commercial in the background. Bright happy voices. But he pulls up a chair and sits.

"Got something on my chest and you guys need to hear it. About Delia. You guys don't know the whole story."

He sips his Pepsi. Okay, she's got his attention.

"I'm a bad mom. I'm a bad mom and I . . ."

"You're not a bad mom," his father says. "I *had* a bad mom. You're not a bad mom."

"Let me talk. I'm a bad mom. That's what I've been thinking ever since Delia got burned up the way she did. I'm a bad mom for making her work instead of going to school. I'm a bad mom for making her work after the fire. Delia and I . . . that morning . . . I don't know how much you guys have noticed but I've been on edge . . . all that travel . . . taking care of Delia's burns . . . Pearl . . . goddamn Pearl . . . that bitch is crazy, you know what I'm saying? But it's not about Pearl, it's about me. What I've been doing. What I've done."

She drinks down her scotch. His father refills it from the bottle of Dewar's on the table. They aren't even bothering with ice.

"Thank you, Bart. I just got so caught up. Trying to keep us afloat. I mean, we were about to go under. Right, hon?"

His father doesn't answer.

"I didn't stop to think about . . . the effects of all this . . . until after that first day with Pearl. I could see Delia was getting more agitated. More confused, more defiant, if you know what I mean. Hell. Why wouldn't she be? I drag her around like a ragdoll, let 'em point cameras at her, hot lights, microphones, all of it. And we collect the checks, right? I say *we*, but I'm the one who calls the shots, right?"

His can of Pepsi is sweating in his hand. He takes a drink. As though on cue, so do they. She runs her tongue over her lips.

"But that morning . . . Delia . . . that morning . . . I just blew my top. I . . . you guys had already left and it was just me and Delia and Caity, just us, eating a quick breakfast. Grapefruit and toast. And the light was coming through the patio window. It was shining on Delia, shining on her face. Her poor, poor face. She was so . . . damaged. And I was feeling guilty I guess and I laid it all on her. Because she'd been so good, we both knew she'd do her job, no matter what, the show must go on, y'know? So I went off big-time, laid it all on her just like I'm doing now only worse. Much worse. I'm a rotten mother. An overbearing stage bitch. All the fucked-up stuff I did . . . I do . . . I am. I got angry. Angry at me. I was yelling, even."

She shakes a cigarette out of the pack and tosses the pack on the table. Uses her lighter and tosses that too. Inhales deep.

"Caity stood up. She was watching me. But Delia just sat there. While I let it all out. She didn't cry. She wasn't afraid. She just watched me and listened. And when I was done . . . I was shaking . . . she put her little hand on mine. She put her little hand on mine and she said, 'It's okay, mom. I don't think all those things about you. I know you care about me and dad and Robbie and Caity. We're family. The TV stuff, the book, all of that's for us. So we'll be okay.' She said she'd been thinking about it all night, how she'd been such a brat lately, her life wasn't so bad. She thought about other kids, kids who didn't have anything in their boring lives. She said that we can tell people what makes our lives so good, what makes us a family. Whatever we have to go through."

He glances at his father. His father seems riveted. Drink nearly gone and poised in midair in front of him.

"She was so strong. She squeezed my hand. My little girl. She said that we had to go on just like we were doing. Go on with the book, go on with the charity. That the charity was important. Really important. I hugged her so tight. And then we just . . . started laughing. She got up and ran away, wrestling with Caity, they were having so much fun. And then . . . and then we had to go and . . . the rest . . . well . . . you know the rest. Merciful god . . ."

He can hear laughter from the TV in the living room. Some sitcom. For a moment nobody moves. She stubs out her cigarette in the ashtray. Wipes her eyes of tears.

"So what I'm saying is," she says, "*it's the charity, the book.* We need to run the charity. Promote the book. For all those kids out there she touched and all those parents of all those kids. You see? You understand? *We need to run the charity.* For her. For Delia. What she would have wanted. For our little girl."

His father sets down his drink and nods. She nods slowly back.

But he can only sit there, staring—at her, at the wall and cupboard behind her until they seem to blend together, woman and surroundings, into one flat surface. And it's as though his sister has spoken to him as clearly as if she were there in the room, listening just as he's been. Has heard everything he's heard.

She's lying, his sister seems to say.

Every word of it, she says.

A lie.

They haven't replaced the window screen but have left the window open just a crack. However a crack is enough for a dog to get through.

She pushes with her snout and then with the top of her head and finally with her front paws against the sill and her shoulders against the sash and then she is outside, where their blanket lies welcoming with softness and scent.

She lies down and there are stars above and a desolate empty space beside her. The night is warm, the air still. There are crickets in the yard. In better days she has been known to eat a cricket now and then, to snatch them out of the air mid-hop.

She yawns and stretches and soon she is asleep.

She awakens to a voice.

Look! Look!

She knows this voice, knows this voice so well. Her tail begins to thump. Her mouth opens, tastes the air. Catches the scent. She gazes up.

Something is moving up there. No, two somethings.

Two hair-thin trails of light, falling slowly, evenly, gracefully toward the earth and toward one another high above, amid the pinprick patterns which are as familiar to her now as the blanket and the gentle slope of roof on which she lies. Two beams converging and then for a moment, joined together in the moonless night.

"Look!" *says the voice again.* "Stars. Shooting stars!"

She watches as they veer apart, as they resume their isolate trajectories down. But the voice does not disjoin from her as these stars do from one another. The voice remains. The voice a part of her now. It belongs to her. It is her own, second voice.

It murmurs in her ear. It laughs. She laughs.

A weight lifts away.

She stands and barks, full-throated and booming from deep down in her chest and barks again. She's calling out. Reaching out. She cannot contain her joy. She announces to the stillness, to the crickets, to the stars.

We are here. We together. We are not alone.

Robbie has no idea what wakes him, only that he jolts wide awake. He can remember no nightmare. He doesn't have to pee. He looks at the illuminated hands of the clock. *Four-ten in the morning.* Less than three more hours and he has to get up for school. He rolls over and closes his eyes but sleep won't come.

Maybe if I eat something, he thinks.

He rolls out of bed and pads barefoot down the hall and down the stairs, quietly so as not to wake his mom and dad, across the foyer into the kitchen and into a scene of utter devastation, illuminated solely by the light from the wide-open refrigerator and freezer doors.

In front of him lies a frozen roast, a package of hot dogs and a package of pork chops, also frozen, two trays of ice cubes, their contents scattered across the floor amid a spray of potato chips in an irregular stream depending from a ravaged plastic bag lying empty against a leg of the kitchen table, and a quart of Häagen-Dazs chocolate ice cream, into the open end of which Caity's muzzle roots greedily.

At his approach she looks up and bares her teeth in what he can only think of as a brown-toothed, brown-faced grin.

"Caity!"

He laughs and she huffs and goes right on back to work.

He's been told never to use the word but he can think it.

What the *fuck*?

He stuffs the roast, chops, and hot dogs back in the freezer, grabs a Pepsi and a bag of pretzels and sits watching until she's through and then cleans up the kitchen floor with mop and broom and goes back upstairs to bed.

Sleeping? No problem.

Pat's still dead to the world but Bart's at the sink all showered and getting ready to go. There's a personal ad in the *Times* for a 2014 Firebird with only two thousand plus miles on it—the price stunning, absolutely nothing for this area—and he's always bitterly regretted the sale of the Red Baron back when times were looking desperate, before Manny Choi picked up the tab for all those bills.

He's going to check it out. It's about fifty miles away but who cares. Nice morning for a drive.

Pat says he likes his toys too much. Well, fuck that. So he likes his toys. So what?

And he needs to cheer himself up, doesn't he?

He's halfway through his shave, working the upper lip toward the chin.

When this *dog* appears in the mirror.

On her hind legs, front paws on the sink. Tongue lolling and tail going like mad. Caity making direct eye contact with his reflection in the mirror. He has to smile.

This is a first.

"Whatchu doin', girl?"

She gives him one of those little pleasure-whines. The kind he'll get when he offers her a treat.

"You want a shave?"

Damned if she doesn't shake her head *no*. That's sure what it looks like, anyway.

He pats her head. She drops to all fours and trots away out the door.

He finishes his shave.

Rrrufff!

Not loud, but loud enough to wake her. Wake her to a splitting headache and limbs that feel like lead.

"Jesus, Caity."

She's prancing in the doorway.

"You want to eat? You want to go out? Go ask daddy. Ask Robbie. Go ask . . ."

She pulls a pillow over her head and drifts back to sleep.

The screen door's swinging shut behind him when Caity comes barreling through. Surprises the heck out of him. Runs right up beside him, keeping pace as he hurries toward the bus stop. She never does that. Always knows to stay inside.

She runs circles around his legs. All excited. Robbie stops and stoops and pets her.

"What? You want to go to school with me? Huh?"

He's running late. If he misses the bus he's going to have to ask his dad for a ride. He doesn't want to do that. More ribbing from the guys. But if he doesn't take her home again how is she supposed to get back inside? He can't just leave her out here. Too bad dogs didn't have opposable thumbs.

"C'mon, girl," he says and takes off toward the house at a fast jog, the heavy schoolbooks sliding side to side into his shoulder blades inside his backpack. Should have packed them tighter, he thinks. But who knew?

He opens the screen door and she just stands there looking at him. Tail drooping. He knows what that means.

"Hey," he says. "I'll be back soon, I promise. You'll hardly even know I was gone. We'll mess around out back. Okay?"

Hesitantly she steps inside.

She punches speed dial. We can hear the phone ringing on the other end.

"Hi, Caits," she says and phone in hand, slides open the glass door. The late-morning sun glares through. "Want to go out and play?"

We sit. We need to pee a little. But we'd rather listen.

She shrugs. "Suit yourself."

Pickup. Roman's voice. Flat, dull, angry.

"What."

"Hi," she says.

"What do you want, Patricia?"

"Bitterness, Roman?"

"I'm going to go on ahead and send you your contact list, my copies of the contracts, headshots, etcetera. Hard copy. Courier can have them there by three."

"Oh, stop. Bart was just trying to impersonate a man in front of his family. We'll work it out."

A long pause. We can hear him breathing.

"I didn't sleep last night."

"I could have helped you with that."

"I thought. A lot. About you. About us. About your kid. It's fucked up, Pat. You're fucked up."

"Roman, who wouldn't be? After what I've been through? Come on."

A sigh. "Your files and things will be there after lunch. If you need anything else from our office, call my assistant."

"Fine. Before you go, though. I need Pearl's office number."

"Why?"

"Did you think I was finished here, Roman? Pretty short-sighted of you, sweetie. Aren't you agents supposed to think ahead?"

"Fuck you, Pat."

"That's your job, cowboy. Number, please."

There's a robin on the patio, pecking away at something. We could chase it. Stretch our legs. We'd rather listen.

Ringing. Receptionist. Then Pearl. Morning, Patricia and good morning, Pearl and so sorry for your loss dear and thank you, Pearl.

"The reason I'm calling. We need to finish this."

"Finish what, darlin'?"

"What we started. Look. Different people deal with things differently. If I just sit around this house, I'm gonna end up hurting myself. I'm not gonna to do that. I want to go ahead."

"Okay. I'm listening."

"This . . . what happened . . . isn't the ending. It's bigger than that. There's a whole third act."

Intake of breath. "Third act?"

"Yes. You already have acts one and two. The dog saves the young girl from a terrible fire, though the dog is burned and the girl is horribly disfigured. Act one. The girl refuses corrective surgery in favor of looking exactly the way she is, staying exactly as she is—a public act of integrity and courage. She starts a charity, Delia's Mirror, writes a book. Act two. Then . . . the girl dies. An awful, unforeseeable accident. But the charity continues, the charity grows, even after the girl's tragic death. Her mother goes on the road in her place. Promotes the charity. Promotes the book. Of which you have a significant piece, remember? Act three."

A long pause and then a laugh.

"You really are a piece of work, Patricia Cross. You know that?"

"What were your ratings on the show we did together? They were through the roof, weren't they."

"Yes, they were. I'll think on it, darlin'. I promise you that."

"Please do."

"Can we still get the dog?"

"Of course we can get the dog. I can do this, Pearl."

"I know you can, honey. I'll get back to you. You be good, now. And you have a nice day."

Roman's pissed.

Screw the courier service. He isn't paying for some goddamn courier service. He climbs in his Jaguar XF. He's driving over.

Call her first? Nah. Fuck it.

Nobody on the winding road but him. A bright sunny day. Life is good. A man feels strong on a day like this. Screw the Cross family. He pulls into their driveway.

He knocks but nobody answers. He tries the door. It's open. He lets himself in.

"Patricia! Bartholomew?"

No answer. He can hear music coming from upstairs, the heavy thump of a bass line, some synthesizer eighties disco shit. *Patricia.* He dumps the box of papers and photos on the coffee table.

What was it she'd said? *That's your job, cowboy.* She sees his job as fucking her. Sure she does. Agent, sure. Partner, sure. Up till now, anyway. But also her fuck-toy. Patty likes it hard sometimes. Well fine, she'll damn well get it hard. One last bareback good-bye fuck from her rodeo cowboy and maybe he'll slap the shit out of her too while he's at it, he'd like that, that would be good, damage that pretty little face of hers just enough for Bart to wonder what the hell happened.

Give makeup something to seriously do for a change.

He heads for the staircase. And stops.

As Caity slides around the corner from the dining room and plants her ass right in front of him at the base of the stairs.

Like she's been waiting for him. Comes out of the room like a shadow.

And maybe he's nuts. But it looks like the goddamn dog is glaring at him. No blink. Just an in-your-face thousand-yard stare.

He knows the dog doesn't like him but fuck that and fuck her, if it comes to a confrontation that's what boots are for and he's wearin' them. Try nice first, though, he thinks. Flies with sugar.

"Hiya, Caity. Hiya, girl."

He's going up. Dog or no dog.

He moves closer but then stops again when over the pounding bass and whirly synthesizer he hears the low growl that seems to dwarf the music and vibrate the very air around him. Low down and dirty mean. Steps one step back when she bares her teeth. Big fuckin' teeth.

Somehow the boots don't seem like such a great idea.

Then she throws back her head and *howls*.

He'd heard wolves howl nights as a kid at his uncle's house along the Oklahoma border but that was outside and scary enough as it was to send him to his mother's bedside crawling into her lap but this is *inside* the fucking house and proximity makes it a whole lot worse and it scares his country ass down to the bone.

Above him the music stops dead. And time seems to stop dead too as she lowers her head and growls again and there's that stare and she's agitating on her haunches so that he realizes she's preparing to move, she's going to move on him, she's going to strike with those great big teeth so he turns and runs like hell for the front door and hears Pat call his name as the door slams shut behind him.

Pat's on the staircase in an instant as soon as she hears that ungodly sound from down below, standing there on the landing half-dressed in bra and silk slip as she watches Roman scramble out of the house with the dog, Caity, hard at his heels until she skids to a stop at the door and Pat calls first his name and then, furious—taking the stairs two at a time—hers.

"Caity! Goddammit! Damn you, Caity!"

The dog's head snaps back. Freezes her in her tracks.

There's a look in her eyes she's never seen before and has never expected to see in a million years, an anger that more than matches her own. The dog's gaze pins her there. She can't move for the life of her. She begins to tremble. It's not the cold.

She hears Roman's car squeal out of the driveway.

Caity sits.

Slowly, the coiled muscles seem to relax. The eyes grow softer. She blinks and blinks again.

And then she trots over. Sits in front of her and looks up into her eyes. It's her *I want to be petted* look. *Pet me.* She knows it well.

To hell with that.

She isn't having it. Her hands are still shaking.

No pets for you, bitch, she thinks. Fuck you. She turns and stalks back up the stairs.

The dog doesn't follow.

Toot-toot. Toot-toot-ta-toot.

He pulls into the driveway, happy as a clam.

How happy *is* a clam, anyway? And why?

Bart loves this car. It isn't the Red Baron, no, instead it's a dark-chocolate-brown but a beautiful bird it is, its owner has cared for it well and the poor sonofabitch must have been way down on his luck, he got it for a song.

He toots again and Pat comes to the door and so does Caity, pouncing out in front of her and bounding across the lawn, Caity delighted to see him and he, just then, delighted to see her too, delighted with everything on this fine sunny afternoon until, as he eases open the driver's side door, she hits the door with her front paws and he hears the long *screeetch* of her nails across the beautiful chocolate high-gloss finish.

"*Fuck, Caity!*" he yells and pushes the door violently open all the way so that she falls to her side onto the driveway with a yelp, landing on her shoulder and he feels guilty about it instantly because it must have hurt but he's pissed off too, dammit, his brand-new car, his brand-new baby, and he stoops to examine it as she stands on unsteady legs and seems to examine him too.

He wipes at the door. The pale white marks come away easily beneath his sleeve.

Not a problem, thank god. A little polish is all.

He turns and raises a hand to her.

"Sorry, Caits. I'm sorry, babe."

She backs away. Then turns and plods weary-looking toward Pat and the open door.

Pearl wants to see the dog so she's brought the dog. And thinking on it, it's probably a very good idea, it'll work with what she has to say. What she's told the police and told her family. What she's asked the police to please *not* relate to the press, to which request they've graciously complied.

So that to Pearl and the public at large this will be news.

The dog had resisted the collar and leash at first but not for long and lies seemingly quite content now at her feet at the long mahogany conference table with Pearl at the other end and Kitty, the assistant, seated next to her with ballpoint pen and pad, pert and scrubbed and poised for notes.

"We were just talking air dates," Pearl says. "I'm liking the Tuesday before Thanksgiving."

"What about Kate Hudson and the vegan guy?" says Kitty.

"Bump 'em. Sound good to you, Patricia?"

"Sounds wonderful."

"You go much later in that week, you start getting into people's travel time. Home for the holidays, right? Don't want to do that. We're going to want Bart and Robbie too for this one. The entire family. They going to be okay with that?"

She smiles. "They'll be fine. I can't promise they'll say much. They're not exactly used to the limelight, if you know what I mean."

"They'll say enough. And they've got a good look together. Two of your basic ordinary guys, easy to relate to. They'll complete the picture."

"If you say so."

"'Course it'll be mostly you and me. Your story, your charity. Get you off and running. You ready to run, girl?"

"That I am. But listen, Pearl. About the story."

"Yes?" Pearl is squinting at her, distrustful now all of a sudden. Pat guesses it comes with the territory. In her business you don't like surprises.

"You wanted to see Caity. You want her to be part of this. Well, she *is* part of it. A bigger part than you know."

She pauses for effect. It works.

"Okay. Speak to me."

"This hasn't come out in the press. But Caity *needs* to be a part of it, Pearl. It's her tragedy too. Like, you know . . . a kind of fall from grace."

"Excuse me? How so?"

"It's got to come out. What happened that day. Caity's role in it. I figured, give the story to you."

"I'm not following."

Caity gets up and trots over to Kitty, who smiles and sets the pen on the table and reaches down to stroke her back.

"She likes to hear her name, doesn't she," Kitty says. "Good doggy."

"Well, we all know how she saved Delia from the fire."

"Sure," says Pearl. "So?"

"That morning. The morning of Delia's fall. It *wasn't just an accident. It wasn't just a fall.* It was Caity who knocked her down. Into the car. Into the lid of the open trunk."

Caity whines, ears flat. Kitty stops petting. They look at her.

"*It was Caity who killed her, Pearl.* She saved her from that horrible burning, saved her only to be the cause of her death and my god, oh god! We were so wound up that day and so . . ."

Caity vomits all over Kitty's shoes.

Dimly we feel we've heard something like this before, a memory of another time, in some sad other lifetime, heard but not understood, yet now it's clear what Pat is trying to say and do and the wrongness rises up and pours out of us and Kitty is saying oh! oh! and Pearl is saying jesus! and goddammit! Pat says and rushes to where we back away from the pool of sick in front of

*us and pulls on the collar, wrenching at our neck and hurt and angry we snarl
and turn and snap and there is flesh between our teeth, Pat's wrist smelling of
flowers with the gold bracelet dangling and she kicks us hard between the ribs
and we shout out once and let go.*

"Goddammit! She fucking *bit* me!"

"She didn't break the skin," says Pearl. "You're okay. You'll be okay."

They watch her slink away beneath the table.

"She ever do this before?"

"Never! No. Jesus!"

"Kitty, let's clean off your shoes, girl. Take 'em off and go get
some towels."

She nods and does as she's told.

When they're alone Pearl regards her across the table. She shakes
her head, sighs, gets up, and walks over to the polished cabinetry on
the wall behind her, opens one of the cabinets to a long row of bottles,
selects one and a pair of highball glasses and sits back down again.

"Glenfiddich. You like?"

"I like. Please. Thank you."

She unscrews the bottle cap and pours.

"This true about her pushing her?"

"They were roughhousing. Yes."

Pearl hands her the glass and they drink. She still feels shaky and
there's a dull pulsing circle of ache all along her right wrist.

"And you never told the cops?"

"I told the cops. I asked them not to let on to the media. They
didn't."

"Makes for a good story though, doesn't it."

"In its way, I guess it does, yes."

"So I'll ask you again. Is it true?"

"I told you it was, didn't I?"

"Yes you did. Problem is, I think you're full of shit. I smell lies,
Patricia. I'll tell your story, though. I like a good story. And there's
truth there, about the way the world works, the way it bites you in

the ass sometimes, so to speak. What's that line? *'Never trust the teller, trust the tale,'* And the charity's a pretty good idea. So yeah, I'll help you tell your damn story."

She drinks and then smiles.

"Not sure about having the dog on, though. Have to think on that. I'm not sure Caity likes you."

Pearl reaches down and Pat sees that Caity's moved to her side and lies at her feet. Pearl scratches her ear.

"Not sure about that at all."

SIXTEEN

P ut down the fucking magazine, Bart. I'm telling you. She bit me!"
"She did? You're really serious? Let's see."

He turns down the page on "The Ten Best Cars of 2015" in *Car and Driver* magazine so he can go back to it later—still wondering if, as they seem to be saying and if the Tesla S60 is any indication, electric cars are really the wave of the future—and hauls his feet down off the couch.

"There's nothing to see. It was two hours ago. She never broke the skin. But she fucking bit me, Bart. She's got to go."

"Go?"

"She doesn't work anymore. I want her out of here."

"What are you talking about? Put her down? Bring her to the vet? Over one bite? Kinda drastic, isn't it?"

"No. The vet's no good. But she doesn't *fit the story*, Bart. One minute she's all Miss Contentment, *Happy Dog*, with Delia barely cold in the goddamn ground. And the next minute she's chasing people, biting people, throwing up on somebody's shoes for god's sake. *Nasty Dog*. Neither one works."

She sits down beside him. Leans in close. Sometimes, he thinks, when her eyes start jittering like this, she kind of scares him.

"But *Sad Dog*. Think about it. Dammit, that *does* work. Dog so sad that she runs away. Runs away because the loss is just too much for her, she's hurting too deeply. Without Delia, she's lost."

"You mean, just dump her?"

"Yes. Dump her."

"That's pretty fucking cruel, Pat."

"Life's cruel, Bart, or haven't you been paying attention? Look. There's two outcomes here. One, we keep the dog and she makes us look like fools, prancing around happy all the time or else barfing on peoples' feet or biting somebody. Or two, she runs away. And we've got poetry."

"Dump her. Just like that."

"In the desert. You take a drive into the desert. You go for drives all the time. Just bring her with you and let her go somewhere. Hell, for all you know she might even survive out there, or somebody'll come along and pick her up. Just let nature take its course."

It feels bad. She's their dog, for heaven's sake. Not just Delia's. She's *the family dog*. It might be smart in the long run, the scenario she was proposing, and yes, she might be right, it could play pretty well. They'd get the sympathy vote again for sure. But it still feels mean and bad.

"And you want me to do this when?" he says. *"Now?"*

"Tomorrow morning. After Rob goes to school. He can't know. The boy's too sensitive and he could never keep his mouth shut. He has to believe what the rest of the world believes. She just took off. Ran away. End of story."

"Jesus, Pat."

"Nobody can know. Just you and me."

She takes his hand and gives it a tight squeeze, then simply holds it awhile.

Just you and me. She could always do this to him, he thinks. No matter what.

"In the morning, then," he says. "I don't like it but okay. Fine. If you say so. Pour me a drink, would you? A stiff one. No ice. And you got a cigarette? I'm out."

She smiles.

The voices have stopped. Our body is tired, so very tired. We stare a moment down the hall, then climb the stairs to the bedroom and the open window and what is outside the window is comfort and safety, a single blanket in the cloudy starless night which is truly home in this familiar, once-loved place that no longer is a home, from which so much love has gone. If we could cry, we would. We settle in once again. One last time.

A full moon glows pale and dull behind the clouds.

The moon reminds us.

We have a voice.

Across the street and three doors down at a house painted turquoise a woman sits beneath her porch light, a woman who once waved to us, friendly, from amid a crowd and who looks up from her book now startled, in wonder, as we rise to our lament, as we begin to howl.

He'd found the model online and thought it might be something different for him and it is. No fenders, no grilles, no tailfins, no cockpits, no propellers, no fuselage. No hard edges. Instead, a canopy fringe, spoke wheels, a fitted floor carpet, gas lamps. An eighteenth-century doorless horse-drawn surrey with spindle-back upholstered seats. Minus the horse.

Maybe he'll build a horse out of wood, like those Greeks in *The Iliad*.

It was pricey but worth it. The precise workmanship on the raw tender plywood, the tiny attention to detail along the rails, the spokes of the wheels narrowed down just so—and it's fitting together like a charm.

Whoever designed this cared.

He is easing in the foot-rests with Lady Gaga belting out "Bad Kids" through his headphones when above the thumping bass and *don't be insecure if your heart is pure* he hears it distinct and ghostly outside his window from the rooftop along the other side of the house where Caity and Delia always sat nights and he tears away the headphones and listens, the notes sliding high and mournful as though to surround him in his room, digging deep—and he thinks, I'll build this one for you, Deal. Just for you. I'll make it a beauty.

SEVENTEEN

W e're thirsty but Robbie provides. He sets down his backpack and cleans and rinses the bowl and fills it with cool fresh water.

"There you go, girl."

He remembers the kibble, pours some into another bowl and sets it down. The kibble is welcome. We've refused wet food for days now so he doesn't bother. He hefts the backpack to his shoulder and is out the door.

The house is silent.

When we're finished we go into the living room and lie down on the couch. We try to sleep. We've hardly slept all night. A fly is buzzing against the window. It's a big fly. Sluggish, fat. Its body thumps against the glass, the morning sunlight beckoning. The fly is trapped by its own ignorance, mistaking light for freedom.

We wait for the house to wake.

Way too much to drink last night and I'm getting old, he thinks, I fucking well pay for it these days.

His headache is a three-alarm fire the instant he rolls out of bed and his only consolation is that she'll be paying for it too, she'd had as much as he had. He weaves on unreliable legs to the bathroom and pops three Aleve, slurping water from his equally unsteady hands cupped against the stream and splashes his face and neck while he's at it.

Not enough. Not even close. Hair of the dog is what he needs.

Hair of the dog, he thinks. Jesus.

Is he really going to do this?

It had been Boodles last night and you'd think he'd know better by now, fucking gin could kill you no matter how pure it is so he goes downstairs to the kitchen in his T-shirt and boxers for a Glenmorangie straight up and chases it with a glass of water from the tap. Then another. Pours a second and sips it this time, feeling the headache start to recede and the buzz begin to take its place. He gulps another glass of water and considers coffee but the smell of brewing coffee risks serious nausea.

A shower.

Upstairs she is still asleep. A shower is not going to wake her. He does not want to wake her.

He turns the water on as hot as he can take it and pulls the curtain and steps inside. It occurs to him that he used to do some of his very best thinking in the shower. Prepare for the day, reflect on the day before. He doesn't anymore. He just soaps and rinses and dries and gets the hell out of there. On this particular morning he figures that's maybe all to the good.

Don't think. Just do.

He dresses in a hurry. She groans in her sleep. He goes downstairs.

In the kitchen again he digs out the engraved silver flask and the funnel and fills the flask with a pint of one-fifty-one vodka instead of the Glenmorangie because the flask imparts a harshness to the liquor and you don't ever want to bruise the smooth finish of a decent single malt.

Never mix, never worry is not one of his mottos.

He has to call her three times to the door leading out to the garage *come on, Caity, come on, girl, we're going for a ride* when once is normally quite sufficient and when she finally does appear her tail and ears are lowered and her eyes downcast as though she's done something wrong, her guilty look, but he doesn't want to wonder about that, he just wants this finished, over and done with.

He opens the driver's side door and waits for her to jump up and in as usual. Instead she sits there staring as though unsure, as though the car were something unfamiliar to her.

Weird, he thinks. She loves to ride.

"Go on, girl. Hop in. I'll roll down the window so you can get some of that good fresh air."

She huffs a deep breath and climbs inside over to the passenger side.

He slides in behind the wheel and hits the garage door opener and starts up the car. The Firebird purrs beneath him.

Backing out he gives her a glance. She's looking straight at him. Sweet-looking dog.

Damn.

"Good pup," he says.

As they approach the community gate he presses the console button for the passenger-side window. She sniffs the air but doesn't stick her head outside. Seems focused on the road ahead.

"This is not on me," he says. "Not on me."

All on her, he thinks.

"Hey, we had a good run, didn't we, girl? Don't you think? How many dogs get a run like that, huh? You've been a good dog, Caits. Hell, I wasn't a bad father, was I. Was I?"

He leans over and ruffles the fur around her ears. They drive in silence for a while. Out of the burbs to the strip mall, the convenience stores, the burger and pizza joints. He is aware of a heaviness in his chest, a choking sensation in his throat.

At the gas station and car wash with the big Native American chief statue in front of it and the mini casino in back he slows and makes a left onto the straight empty highway headed through the desert toward the mountains. Nothing out here but a boulder now and then or low sandstone rock studded along the side of the road like jagged teeth in a desiccated bleak skull of sand. It's safe to pull out the flask now so he does. He uncaps it and takes a long pull. The warm vodka burns its way down his throat.

He welcomes the feeling. Has another.

"*You* weren't the bitch in the family, were you?" he says. "We both know who the bitch is, don't we. Hey, I married her!"

Caity's acting strange. She should be hanging halfway out the window by now, enjoying the warm breeze. This road is new to her. She should be curious. Instead she's turned around in the passenger seat, looking back out the rear window. He glances into the rearview mirror, the Big Chief statue fading in the distance.

Another pull. He's seriously feeling it now. It's about fuckin' time.

He considers music. The CD player. The radio. But music doesn't seem right somehow. He takes another hit of the one-fifty-one. Music's wrong. Hell, let's face it, *it's all wrong.*

"Fuck!" he says. "Just dump the damn dog! Do the shit work! Good old Bart. Let him do all the shit work. You know what? I shoulda smacked her, you know that? Right from the start, kept her in line. I fucked up, though. Fucked a lot up. Maybe if I hadn't fucked up, things would've been different for us. You, me, Delia. Shit!"

He pounds the steering wheel. Wipes the tears from his eyes.

"*Weak!*"

He takes another pull. The pint's still about three-quarters full. It'll manage to get him wherever he's going, there and back. Fine.

Caity is looking at him now, not the road.

He slaps the wheel again.

"Why'd you do it, girl? Why'd you have to go and bite the big bad wolf? Damn!"

He sets the pint between his legs and reaches over to stroke her, pet her—their dog, *his* dog—and feels her tense and stiffen at his touch. And it comes to him then. A kind of superstitious dread. A worm of fear inside. He looks into her eyes which look back hard into his and he thinks, *she knows, goddammit, somehow she knows what I'm supposed to do* and he withdraws the hand, the hand seeks out the flask instead, the comfort there as she turns to the open window and begins to scramble through it, her front legs and half her chest already out the window, rear legs off the car seat and pawing for purchase at the arm rest.

"Caity!"

He drops the flask and lunges for her, the reach to her collar too far, impossible, so he grabs for her haunches, her tail, her legs, almost gets hold of one as the car swerves, a crazy thing, as it blurts off the road into cacti and spewing sand and then she's gone, disappeared out the window as his back right tire screeches and lifts against something low and hard and the car spins dizzily and he wrenches at the wheel for control as in front of him through the windshield the boulder looms.

We know the way. Our ears, our nose, our eyes are one single thought and they show us the way. They'll lead us home.

We're thirsty. It's hot.

The road beneath our feet is hot. Too hot. The sand is better. Feet slipping, sliding, but better.

We walk and walk toward the tall statue in the distance and the sun rises farther up the sky and farther still. There are birds high above. Something gray and small scuttles burrowing into the sand beneath a cactus at our approach.

Cars fly by, blowing waves of heat and sand. We turn our eyes away. We walk.

And finally there is the statue and the gas station and car wash and in front of the car wash a small sickly dog is tethered and barks at us, furious, as we pass. At the exit to the strip mall a car halts its turn onto the highway and at the entrance another brakes for us and stops its turning in. We feel this driver's eyes on us as an accusation. We've inconvenienced him. We pay him no mind.

We're going home.

We know the way.

EIGHTEEN

Where's Caity?"

She's always right at the door when he comes in. He's always wondered if she hears the bus or the car or if it's just some doggy sixth sense telling her he's home but whatever it is, she's always right there waiting for him like she's been sitting there forever.

His mom is lying feet-up on the couch in front of the television. Alex Trebek. *Jeopardy.*

"I dunno. With your dad I guess. He was going for a drive. Must have brought her along for the ride."

She's been drinking. He can tell by her voice. Middle of the afternoon and she's still in her bathrobe. The coffee cup on the table in front of her isn't fooling anybody. He knows what's in there.

The place reeks of cigarette smoke. She's chain-smoking too now? He figures he'll open the patio doors and let in some air.

Caity's stuff lies right in front of him. Piled none too neatly just to the left of the doors. Her water bowl, food bowls, a ten-pound bag of kibble and some cans of food, her leash, a pair of thick leather bone-shaped chew-toys, some bright-colored rubber balls, and the little stuffed dragon she likes to toss around every now and then.

What the hell's going on?

He feels blood rush to his head. His heart's pounding.

She'd bitten her.

She wouldn't. She couldn't.

The vet, he thinks. *Put her to sleep. Put her down.*

He storms back into the room.

"Where is she, mom? Why's her stuff out there? Where's my dog?"

She drinks from the cup.

"*Your* dog! Ha! *Delia's* dog. Not yours."

"Where is she? What did you *do*, ma?"

"I didn't do a damn thing. Talk to your father."

"Did you . . . ?"

She slams the cup down on the table. Stands and walks over and gets right in his face.

"I told you. I didn't do a damn thing. I don't have to answer to you."

He could smell her smoke-and-whiskey breath, feel it on his cheek.

"And who the fuck *cares*?"

"I care! Caity's . . ."

Family, he's going to say, but she puts her hand to his chest and pushes him. He backpedals, astonished. She's never hit him, never touched him before. Not like this. He catches his balance.

She's *pushed* him. *Just like she pushed Delia*? Is that possible?

It is.

The word flies out of him. The word surprises him.

"Bitch!"

Her finger stabs his chest. The fingernail filed sharp.

"What? What did you say? Don't you *ever* talk to me like that, you understand me? Not ever! You miserable little . . ."

He's scared, trembling all over but dammit, he's standing his ground on this.

"I want to know what you did, mom! What did you do to Caity? What did you do to my sister."

"What? You little shit!"

He sees the slap coming but he can't dodge it. Some part of him doesn't even want to dodge it.

Let her, he thinks. *Let's see. Let's see who she is.* What she's hiding.

The force of it sends him to the ground, ears ringing, stung all across his cheek and jaw. He lies in front of her on the carpet, blinking his eyes back into focus.

A spider, he thinks. That's what she looks like. Legs spread, arms held wide away from her to either side, fingers spread like claws, back hunched, head and neck protruding off her shoulders like some creature about to strike.

"Get up," she says. "Get the fuck up and go to your room. I see your face down here again tonight you'll get it again, you hear me? You'll get worse. Now get out of my sight. Get!"

He gets up. He does what he's told.

But this? This isn't over.

The nice lady from across the street is on her porch again, rocking, a folder and some papers on her lap in front of her. She sees us—tongue lolling, we can't help it—and stands.

"Hey! Hey, doggie, hey, sweetie, come on, c'mere!"

She motions us over. We hesitate, then trot up the porch steps. She squats and runs her hands over our head, pats our chest.

"Look at you, you're all lathered up! Want some water? Sure you do. Sit. Wait right here. Wait."

She disappears behind the screen door and we look over across the street. We listen. The house stands quiet.

She returns with a bowl of water and a paper towel and wipes the foam from our mouth before she sets it down. We drink. The water's so cold we feel an ache in our chest as it goes down but it's wonderful and we empty the bowl in no time at all. She strokes our head.

"What are you doing out here, anyway, huh? Let's get you home," she says.

She takes hold of our collar as though to guide us.

It's not necessary. We know where we're going.

"My dog Caity. Did my dad . . . did my dad bring her in?"

He can hear a dog barking in the background. Sharp and shrill. Not Caity.

Their vet's receptionist asks if she can put him on hold and he says yes and then waits holding his breath, afraid to breathe, while some Muzak version of "Bridge over Troubled Water" plays tinny in the background and then she's on the line again.

"No, Robbie. They haven't been in today. Is there anything I can help you with?"

"No. Thanks. 'Bye."

He hangs up the phone in their bedroom relieved but thinking, *now what?* and hears the doorbell ring downstairs.

"Look who I found!"

"What the . . . ?"

The woman is smiling, their neighbor, Leda, the newsperson, the anchor for god's sake. She lets go of the collar and the dog trots past her to the foot of the stairs and sits.

She's aware that her mouth is open. She closes it.

Put on the face, she thinks. *Pleasure and astonishment.*

The astonished part is easy.

"How did you . . . ? Where did you . . . ?"

"She came right on up to the house. I gave her some water."

"Well, god, thank you! I have no idea how she . . ."

"She was awfully thirsty."

"Thank you so much. I had no idea she'd gotten out."

"Well, she's home safe now, isn't she."

203

"Yes. Thank you. Thank you so much."

"My pleasure."

The woman looks on past her to the staircase and waves and smiles again. Pat looks over her shoulder. To Robbie standing on the landing.

"You folks have a good day, now!" she says.

"You too. Thanks again."

She quietly closes the door.

"What?" she says. "You happy now?"

What the hell is going on, she thinks. Where the hell's Bart? What's the goddamn dog doing here?

She doesn't like the way the dog is just sitting there, looking at her. She doesn't much care for the expression on her son's face either. Screw the both of them.

"Caity! C'mon, girl," Robbie says.

The dog turns and climbs the stairs.

"Fuck this," she says. She sits back down on the couch and drains the bourbon in her coffee mug, digs the cell phone out of her bathrobe pocket, and speed-dials Bart's number. She gets his voicemail after a single ring. Redials and gets it again. Then a third time.

"*Goddammit!" Where the hell are you, Bart?"*

She slams the phone down on the coffee table. It immediately begins to ring.

The display reads *Saint Agnes Hospital.*

"Yes?"

"Mrs. Cross?" A woman's voice. Young, she thinks.

"Yes?"

"I'm sorry. I'm afraid I have some bad news for you, Mrs. Cross. There's been an accident. Your husband's been very badly hurt. We have him here in intensive care. You'll want to get over here as soon as possible. Do you know where we are, ma'am?"

"Hurt?"

"Yes, ma'am. Do you know where we are?"

"Yes. Oh yes. Believe me, I know where you are. Thank you."

She slams the phone down a second time.

Impossible, she thinks. *How in god's name?* And then she thinks, go get dressed. Get the hell over there.

Her son and dog are watching from the stairs.

"What? What are *you* looking at?"

Like they're accusing her. Like they have the *right* to accuse her.

She tromps up the stairs. On the landing Robbie scoots over but the dog doesn't, the dog just sits there.

In my way, she thinks. *You're always in my goddamn fucking way, aren't you.*

I'll move your ass.

She reaches down and grabs her by the collar, grips it hard, sees Robbie flinch away beside her and then turns, whirling.

And hurls the goddamn dog down the stairs.

The dog yelps, tumbling end over end and skittering along her side but then catches herself, finds her legs on the third step from the bottom, steadies herself glaring up at Pat, and she has a single terrible moment to regret what she'd done, impulsive, violent, and stupid, which is not like her at all, not the way she thinks of herself whatsoever, before the dog charges snarling back up the stairs.

She runs for the bedroom, the door she can close behind her and there it is, it's right there in front of her and she reaches for it as the dog's teeth sink into the meat of her calf and jerk her foot out from under her and she falls screaming in pain and her fear turns to sudden blinding fury so that she pivots on her hip and bends forward from the waist and reaches out thumbs–first to the dog's eyes, *into* the dog's eyes, gouging at the dog's eyes so that it yips and draws away and she kicks it with her bloodied leg hard in the snout.

She is on her feet and through the doorway thinking, get to the phone, the police, call the police, and shoves the door hard behind her and hears it slam against the doorjamb but it doesn't engage, the damn thing does that sometimes, you have to press it home, and then hears it slam against the wall which means the dog is inside. She doesn't look back.

The bathroom. Lock the door.

A fine idea except that the dog is faster than she ever might have guessed, faster than she's ever seen it move before, heading her off, racing over the bed and onto the vanity table scattering lotions and pills and perfume bottles crashing every which way and then leaping off the vanity to the floor in front of her. Her feet go out from under her as the throw rug sails away across the floor and she lands on her ass in front of the table with the flat-screen perched on top like a bird of prey looming down at her.

The dog barks and snaps its teeth, haunches trembling with excitement.

She grapples for the table, uses the table to try to haul herself up but the angle's wrong, her weight's too much. The table tilts, falling, the flat-screen along with it and she senses the screen's trajectory and tries to scuttle crabwise away but feels it crash down across her shins and she screams in pain as the dog pounces directly on top of the thing, snapping, snarling, drool spraying across her face.

She pushes with all her strength and screen and dog go flying. She crawls toward the bathroom through the high reek of lotion and perfume and broken glass from the vanity, feels glass pierce the palms of her hands and knees and then her hands find the sink and she's begun to drag herself up when the dog's teeth clamp down on the toes of her left foot, she hears the crunch of bone even before she feels it and she screams again and falls, her jaw slamming the rim of the tub and she's bitten her tongue, the taste of warm blood putrid in her mouth and she turns to her back and kicks and kicks at the dog with both feet, blood flying off her foot, kicks until she catches its snout again directly, perfectly, and the fucking thing yelps bright and sharp and runs whining from the room.

She hears the patter of the dog's feet in the hall and then there's silence except for her own heavy breathing. Waves of pain wash over her body. She looks down at her mangled foot. The big toe hangs loose at a wholly unnatural angle. She listens to the silence. Swallows blood. Listens for the dog. Listens and then thinks *where the hell's Robbie?* Where's her son?

She uses the sink and carefully, quietly, lifts herself off the bathroom floor.

From where he stands on the landing Robbie hears it all, Caity barking, snarling, his mother screaming, breaking glass, and something heavy falling, and the sounds repel and beckon to him, both at once. He inches along the wall toward their bedroom until he's standing at his own doorway, terrified to go further.

He hears Caity yelp and hears her claws *tick tick tick* across the bedroom floor and then she's out there in the hall stopped and staring up at him. There's blood along her mouth and nose but it's her eyes which draw him, her eyes which hold him. The eyes are that same deep, dark familiar brown he's known for years but what's in them, what resides inside the eyes is not the same at all. Though it, too, is familiar.

And impossible.

He leans forward from the wall, the better to see.

His sister and he were twins. Not nearly identical, but close enough. Especially around the eyes.

He sees pity there and a great and terrible longing.

"Delia?" he says. "*Deal?*"

Impossible.

The hall begins to slide and swim. So that when his mother storms raging, limping out of the bedroom with the heavy ceramic lamp from atop their dresser raised in both hands high above her head, naked inside the parted robe, teeth bared in a bloody snarl, it's too much, way too much, and as Caity turns to meet her he throws himself inside his room and slams the door.

The lamp is a bad idea. Clunky fucking thing with too much weight to it but it was the first thing that came to mind, the first thing at hand, she should have stripped a curtain rod or the shower rod, telescoped it down, cracked it like a whip. But all she could think of was to hurt the damn thing, kill the fucking thing for what it's done—her leg, her foot, the glass in her hands and knees—and the dog launches itself at her and *bitch!* she screams as sixty pounds of muscle hit her in the chest and even as she brings the lamp down across its withers she knows it's not nearly enough and the lamp falls away from her hands as she hits shoulder-first against the wall behind her, smashing Delia's first framed headshot to the floor. The dog backs away from the skittering broken glass and that moment is all she needs to throw open the door to Delia's room.

Delia's iPad still rests on the nightstand by the bed. She dives for bed and iPad at the same time and as the dog leaps up to straddle her on the bed, turns and rams the tablet into the side of its head. The dog reels, falling off the bed but it's back on her in an instant, snapping at her face while she batters at its shoulders, back, and head and feels herself weakening, ineffectual, *useless*, the two of them eye to eye, Pat unable to look away as the dog moves effortlessly up her body, takes her lower jaw into its own jaws, clamps down, and *pulls.*

The sound that escapes her as her jaw rolls and disjoints is unlike anything she's ever heard before or thought she could possibly make, a high-pitched stuttering wail of sound, like machine-gun fire ricocheting in this tiny room, sliding down octaves to a roar, then to a low moan through the seeping welter of blood which pools at her collarbone

The dog releases her and there's that stare again, the stare that has so enraged her on the landing but it isn't rage she's feeling now but only pain and terror and her hand goes to her exposed neck. She's aware of the dog's weight along her body, her thighs, her exposed bloody breasts.

Then it releases her, rises up on all fours, alert, the bed trembling beneath them.

It gazes around the room. Suddenly still but for its breathing. As though the dog were seeing the room for the first time. Its eyes roam.

It begins to whine as if in pain, as though the dog were hurt and bleeding here and not her.

Its eyes narrow. It growls. Jumps off the bed.

And then it's in Delia's closet, standing on its hind legs and tearing at the clothes inside, tearing them off the hangers to the floor. Dresses, blouses, costumes, a straw bonnet, a beaded handbag, ripping them down and savaging them, snarling, on the bedroom floor. *Auditions, performances.* Her daughter's past torn to pieces here in front of her.

Patricia—for the moment—forgotten.

A breeze on her cheek through the open window.

The roof.

She crawls across the bed. Shards of glass dig deeper into her hands as she grips the windowsill and wrenches herself into the open air. Behind her all sounds cease. She has her left leg over the sill, its ruined toe curling back on itself as it touches the roof and she screeches in pain into the dimming evening sky.

She feels the weight of the dog hit the bed, she pulls her right leg free of both room and dog and whirls in sudden intuition and slams the window down behind her and hears it *thunk* against the dog's back, the dog howling, half in and half out the window so she pushes it down harder still thinking, *got you, bitch,* and turns toward the tree, the tree the dog had climbed years ago it seems, in another world amid smoke and flame.

She reaches into the branches and grips one, stout and steady, lets her feet drop off the roof and then she's hanging there, legs swinging, going hand over hand as best she can, not built for this, jerking her body toward the trunk of the thing but there's blood on her hands, her hands are slick with it and she feels herself slipping, fingers like talons but sliding down anyway over the rough, sap-smelling wood.

She feels the weight of her body clawing her to earth and at last her hands give way and she tumbles free fall through the tree, its branches knife blades, razors, hammers. She glimpses the spread of roots and grass rising fast below, skewed to one side as her body takes one final turn and then sees nothing at all.

You need to do something, he thinks. *Now.* You need to stop hiding. You need to go to her. But exactly who he needs to go to he's not exactly certain.

He flings open his bedroom door. In the hall Caity's howl shudders through his body. He has barely a second to register Delia's torn clothes strewn across her room before he sees Caity struggling at the window, trapped, arching her back, rear paws scrabbling for purchase against the wall. He throws himself across the bed, takes her hindquarters under one arm and rams the window open with the other. She yelps in freedom. Reaches up and licks his face, his chin, his lips. But she wants down.

He lets go.

She tears across the bedroom floor and down the stairs and he follows. She whines in frustration as her front paws scratch uselessly at the double glass doors and then she does the most amazing thing, something he's never seen her even attempt to do before. She raises her right front paw, wedges her claws between the door and the doorjamb, shifts the bulk of her body and simply *pushes.*

The door slides open. Caity is outside.

She awakens to pain and utter clarity. The dog has somehow gotten free, the fucking dog is streaking toward her across the lawn. She bolts upright to her feet and instantly finds her balance, screw the pain and *fuck you, dog, you're dead!* burning like a fever.

The dog flings itself up at her and her timing's perfect, a dancer's timing, a dancer's perfect balance too as heedless of her ruined foot she steps to one side and the dog goes hurtling past her head first into the metal slide behind her. Before the dog can right itself her hands are tight around its neck and she slams the head down to the rim of the slide and dog seems almost to scream with pain, an almost human sound—wonderful, exalting—and she slams it down again. The dog goes limp in her hands and she lets it fall.

She stumbles onto the patio and there's Robbie standing just inside the doorway.

"*Useless,*" she mutters, "you get the *fuck* out of my way," and she shoves the useless little prick as hard as she can, her fury in no way abated, fury at the dog, at him, at Bart, at the whole miserable shithole of a world and hears him tumble into the kitchen chairs and table and doesn't even turn to look.

She's getting the hell out of there. Through her own goddamn front door to her own goddamn street.

She's never loved anybody, nobody, not a soul, it was all a lie, he thinks as the arm of the chair gouges his eye and cracks his nose and he slides down across the cold kitchen tiles.

She's halfway across the living room marching like the soldier she is and has always been when the dog's front teeth crush through the palm of her right hand and its back teeth pulp her thumb and index finger and pull her to the floor.

The dog shakes the thumb free. She sees it, hears it, drop to the floor.

Blood spurts across the muzzle of the dog, across her, across the sofa and she thrashes at it, slapping at the thing, screaming at the thing, thinking crazily *you were supposed to die! you're supposed to be dead god-dammit!* as the dog hunkers down and appears to listen—to what she has no idea, but not to her, somehow she knows that—to something deep inside its unknowable brain perhaps, yet she thinks she sees sad-ness, yes sadness in its eyes for a moment as it pauses above her but then it rears and darts forward and its teeth find her throat as she has known they would and an arc of blood pulses far and wide and pulses again as the dog jerks its head back and something breaks inside her so that when she looks down she sees something stubby, white, a tube of some sort, glistening, flecked with blood and surrounded by bright raw flesh depending from her neck, leaning like a finger toward her collarbone.

The room turns red, blood in her eyes that she has no will, no strength to wipe away. She sees Robbie standing over her, leaning heavily on the arm of the sofa and thinks she sees a phone in his hand—it's definitely a phone, a cell phone—and she tries to say *call, call somebody* but it doesn't sound like that, it sounds wrong.

And she thinks, who would he call anyway.

He can't watch her. Can't watch the blood pool around her shoul-ders, neck, and head. Can't watch her die although he knows it, feels it when she does. He has the phone in his shaky bloodstained hand, he's punched in the first two digits of 911 almost automatically when through the swarm of thoughts and feelings a single one emerges like a drowning man gasping to the surface.

My god. Caity. Delia.

They kill a dog for this.

Blood still seeps from his nose so he wipes it with the bottom of his *How To Kill A Zombie* T-shirt which is already so stained from the initial spurt and steady drip that it looks like blood is part of the design.

His blood. Not hers.

He considers this.

He has a bloody nose. And judging by the tenderness beneath his right eye, if he doesn't have a shiner by now it won't be long before he does.

He thinks it through. And yes, he can call 911. He can.

He knows what to say.

They'd argued. It got violent. He'd confronted her with his suspicions, that it was her, his mom, not Caity, who was responsible for his sister's death and she denied it at first, got furious with him, then finally confessed and when she did she went crazy, went after him either to shut him up, prevent him from telling or out of guilt or something, he doesn't know, only that she went after him and gave him this black eye and this bloody nose and he was afraid she'd push him down the stairs, afraid for his life, he thought she was going to kill him too just like Delia but then Caity came between them, Caity went after *her*, Caity rescued him, if it weren't for Caity god knows what she'd have done.

You can do this, he thinks. You can make them believe it. They *have to* believe. Caity's already a hero dog, isn't she? Everybody knows that. He even thinks Pearl might back him up. And not just about Caity. He thinks that Pearl might have her own suspicions about his mother too.

So quiet, he thinks. The house is so weirdly quiet. Like a thunderstorm just passed.

Where is she? Where's Caity? He hadn't been able to look at her either. *After.*

He finds her waiting by the water dish. The water dish is empty. He fills it from the sink. When she's done he fills it again.

Then he dials 911.

We sit in the bathtub. The water's warm.

Robbie's got the handheld showerhead, washing away the blood. And with it, the pain.

The soap smells wonderful.

We can hear sirens in the distance. But they're off a ways yet. We have time. We wonder if Robbie can hear them or if it's only us.

There's a tiny sliver of glass in our right front paw wedged between the pads. We hold it up to him. He gets a tweezer from the medicine cabinet and gently pulls it free.

We kiss him in that way dogs do.

He wipes his face and smiles. The first we've seen him smile all day.

"Thanks, sis," he says.

We kiss him once again.

"We're losing him!" says the man in white hovering above him and instantly the man is gone, his daughter's face, her unburned face small and round and smiling is there instead and Bart feels something cold and wet against his chest and thinks *I'm sorry, sorry for everything* and the world turns to sparks of flame and darkness all around.

EPILOGUE

H appy Halloween!"
Aunt Ev sounds great as usual, hale and hearty. Rob thinks she'll probably live to be a hundred, that woman, even though arthritis has driven her finally to leave the place outside Hamburg, his place now, and move to a smaller home in Sparta, one-story, so she doesn't have to climb "those darn stairs." They kid her about moving to the Great Big City, which by Sussex County standards, Sparta is.

She asks after the family and he sips his cup of coffee and tells her all is well. He gazes through the double glass doors in the kitchen out past the fieldstone patio to a pair of squirrels racing around the wheels of the wooden eighteenth-century auto-top surrey he's found at auction and restored himself, which sits in his half-acre yard, roughly where, in that *other* house, the swing set and slide had been.

Family excepted, he guesses the surrey's his pride and joy. After all, it had been that long-ago model with the spindle-back seats he'd made for Delia which had got him interested in antiques in the first place. Then when Evvie took him in, practically the entire house was furnished in American Country, some of it in pretty bad shape. Rob found he had a knack for fitting and gluing, for repair. Building models—those he hadn't tromped to death in his frequent fits of pique—had taught him meticulousness and patience.

He has his own business now, he and Ana. Their own shop out back off the driveway at the edge of the ten acres of woods that horseshoe the property, and a permanent stall among the almost forty other dealers and restorers at Main Street's Hamburg Antique Center. Ana has a fine hand with the much older stuff, the American Primitive. Their pie safe, the sea chest that doubles as their coffee table, the Windsor chairs, the rolltop desk—they're all her doing.

But it's still the surrey that holds pride of place for him amid all their stuff. In bad weather he'll zip it up in plastic, oust the truck from the garage, and wheel it in against the depredations of rough North Jersey winters and refinish it every spring. In summertime he and Ana take their drinks and sit out there and watch the world go by.

Outside the glass doors—adding them for the light has been their sole alteration to the place—the two squirrels have been joined by a third who sits perched atop the surrey's right front wheel munching something between its paws that looks suspiciously like one of the kids' Dorito chips.

"You all set for some trick-or-treaters tonight?" he asks his aunt.

"Got three boxes of Reese's Pieces. I figure that oughta do 'em."

"Oh yeah? How very *E.T.* of you! They're Charlie's favorite, y'know."

It's Charlie's favorite movie too. His eight-year-old son has a crush on Dee Wallace. Which he thinks shows very good taste on his part.

"'Course I do. Why do you think I bought so many of 'em? Charlie can have the leftovers. Got a box of mini Mars bars too."

"For Stella."

"Yup. For Stella."

"You spoil us, Ev."

"Hey, you turned out okay, didn't you? And I spoiled the bejeezus out of you."

Next to Christmas, Halloween is Ev's favorite holiday. You didn't get many trick-or-treaters out here in the sticks and she'd always said she missed that, but now that she's in town she gets plenty. She loves seeing the kids playing dress up, the monsters and ballerinas and superheros.

Hell, she loves kids, period. She'd proven that with him.

"I found the perfect pumpkin over at John Fee's day before yesterday," he says. "It's sitting right here on the mantel over the fireplace. I can't decide whether to carve it or not. Like I say, it's perfect."

"Carve it. That fresh-cut pumpkin smell, remember?"

"I remember."

"And who the heck wants perfect?"

She reminds him about next Saturday. Boiled New England dinner at her house. Ham, potatoes, and cabbage, and thick-sliced German bread from Manger's Bakery.

"We'll be there. Six o'clock sharp."

"Six o'clock sharp. Go carve that pumpkin. Caity loves the smell."

He smiles. "Yes, Caity does."

At the mention of her name she looks up from in front of the living room fireplace in which three logs smolder and trots over.

"Want to say hello, Ev?"

"Nah. I'll see her on Saturday. Give her a hug for me."

"Will do. Love you, Aunt Ev."

"Love you too, Robbie."

She's the only one in the world still allowed to call him Robbie. To everybody else including his wife he's Rob.

True to his word he hangs up and bends down and gives Caity a hug around the shoulders and a kiss atop her head, ruffles the fur on her chest which has grown back white and silky after the burning so long ago.

Over twenty years ago.

At thirty-two there's already some salt-and-pepper in his hair but not a trace in Caity's. Aging seems somehow to have passed her by.

He'd taken her to a vet once—only once—about two years ago. She'd sprained her ankle in a mole-hole chasing after some rabbit one early summer morning and the limp was bad. He was afraid the leg was broken. The vet was a woman who looked barely old enough to be out of college. But like most folks around here her tongue was sharp and salty.

She listened to Caity's heart and breathing, took her pulse and set down the stethoscope and shook her head.

"I'll be good goddamned if I get it," she said. "Pardon my French. How old did you say this dog is?"

"We don't know exactly. She's . . . a rescue."

"I got to tell you, this dog confuses hell out of me. Her temp's two degrees below normal, her pulse is reading at sixty beats per minute. Which is old-dog slow. But I don't see an old dog here, do you? And her breathing's all wrong. She should be coming in at about twenty-four breaths per minute. Caity's is *twelve*, for god's sake. More like a human than a Queensland Heeler. Never seen a damn thing like it."

And you won't again, Rob thought. But he kept his mouth shut tight on that one.

She x-rayed the leg and diagnosed a sprain, proscribed some anti-inflammatory drugs and told him about ice packs and heating pads and sent him on his way.

"You come back soon now," she said. "Dogs need their regular checkups."

He very much doubts he will. Happily there's never been any need to. He grooms her often, brushes her teeth against tooth decay, feeds her lean human food and kibble, and she never has so much as a sniffle.

He wishes he could say as much for his kids.

Both of whom now burst through the front door, Ana holding it open for them, all three of them loaded down with shopping bags.

"Caity!" says Stella.

"Wiggle-butt!" says Charlie.

Caity lopes over and the kids' packages are abandoned in favor of wet dog-kisses, pets, and hugs. Around Caity, Stella always seems to forget that at nine she's the elder of the two and loses any pretense of her usual, slightly self-conscious, slightly superior dignity.

He helps Ana carry the packages into the kitchen and pile them on the butcher-block table.

"Mission accomplished," she says. "There shall be Halloween!"

She laughs, face flushed from the October chill. That deep throaty laugh, he thinks, was the first thing about her that seduced him his sophomore year at Plymouth State College. He was an English major, for no other reason than, like his aunt, he loved to read—everything from Stephen King to Will and Ariel Durant. She was Languages. She could still read perfectly well in Japanese.

But when they discovered they were both antique-freaks college fell by the wayside. Ev had loaned them most of the cash to set them up in business before they were even married. Prescient, he's always thought, that they would be before too long.

They set to unpacking, groceries first. Häagen-Dazs in the freezer.

"You'll never guess what I just recorded," he says.

"What?"

"Pearl's twentieth-year retrospective. Me at age twelve. The whole family. Promoting that damn book."

"You *swore*, dad. What book? You were *twelve*?"

They haven't even heard her approach. Like her mother, Stella is light on her feet.

Charlie and Caity appear in the doorway behind her.

"That book sent your daddy to college, sweetie," Ana says.

"Want to see what we got, dad?" says Charlie.

"Absolutely."

His son sets to rummaging through the packages on the table. Bags of candy for the trick-or-treaters who probably wouldn't show. Halloween decorations—three orange-and-black cardboard owls, a cardboard skeleton hinged at the joints, a pair of papier-mâché witches on broomsticks, and a plastic toothless jack-o'-lantern for the door. Finally he finds what he wants.

"This one's Stella's," he says.

She tugs the box out of her brother's hands and opens it. Inside is a pretty red fake-velvet costume, complete with leggings and a draped hood. She pulls the hood over her shoulders.

"See? Little Red Riding Hood," she says.

She does a half-turn for her audience. Including Caity, who's up on her hind legs, paws on the kitchen table.

"That's terrific, Stel'," he says. "Do I perhaps see a wolf in this picture?"

Charlie laughs and high-fives him and pulls out a second box. A full-body gray wolf costume. Not *too* high-end, he thinks—they're by no means rich—but not too shabby either. They'll make a fun pair, barreling along in the truck from neighbor to neighbor. Charlie puts on the mask and growls through its feral toothy grin.

Caity barks right back at him.

"Can I have a Twizzler?" Stella asks. "Me and Caity?"

"Just one," he says. "Bad for her teeth."

"How 'bout a FarBar?" says Charlie. "Just me. No Caity."

"Sure. One."

The kids unwrap the candy and Stella hands a cherry Twizzler over to Caity who gets down off the table and sits munching it between her paws, delicate, small bites at a time.

"What book, dad?" says Charlie. "One you wrote?"

"I just talked. Somebody else did the writing. It was . . . about your Aunt Delia."

"*Aunt Delia*? Really?" says Stella. "Can we see?"

Charlie nods enthusiastic agreement. Delia has become something of a family legend to these guys.

He and Ana exchange glances. He wonders yet again when the kids would begin to question what Ana had learned from him and come to accept long ago. Why *this* Caity had the same scars and slashes of pure white fur along her belly, the lightning-bolt from ear to chin, as her supposed mother.

"What do you think?" he says.

"Can't hurt I guess," she says.

"Caity?"

She looks up at each of them in turn. The kids first. Rob last. Then barks and wags her tail. They have permission.

"Okay, leave that stuff, Ana," he says. "Come on, guys. My room. The study. Let's go watch your dad on TV."

He herds them out of the kitchen. Ana smiles at him over her shoulder.

He bends down to Caity. She nuzzles his open hand, his chin.

"Know what I heard on the news this morning?" he says. "No, you were sleeping. Meteor shower tonight. That's right, falling stars. So what do you think? You up for that?"

He kisses her on the forehead.

"Yeah, I thought so," he says. "I was pretty sure you would be."

They rise together and walk on down the hall.

It's night. The house is silent.

Ana lies propped up on two firm pillows, leafing through an issue of Town & Country Magazine. *A boutique hotel in Abruzzo has caught her eye, the bedroom of a medieval house now a cozy place for guests to sleep, its walls aglow like honey, its furnishings simple, spare, and elegant. Not unlike their own home on a bright summer day.*

In their beds, in their separate rooms, Stella and Charlie are asleep. Each, as it turns out, dreams of the other.

In Charlie's dream his sister walks a long wide path through a garden, all reds and blues and yellows. She stops to examine a spiderweb. And in it, the spider. She's not afraid of spiders. Though Charlie is a little afraid for her. She turns to laugh at something far behind her and skips away.

In Stella's dream Charlie has a hammer in his hand and he's breaking through a wall. The wall is thick and Charlie's sweating. It's a lot of work. But her brother doesn't seem to mind. He's purposeful, methodical, finding all the weak spots. And finally there's a hole big enough to peek through. He does, presses his eye blinking to the hole. She has the distinct feeling that she's on the other side.

On the gently slanted roof is a blanket, tattered by now in places, mended and tattered again. But comfortable and familiar as a second skin.

Here two figures sit quiet and content waiting in the stillness and the deep country dark for the sky to starburst above them.

The dust of the heavens, fashioned in violence into bright trails of light.

ACKNOWLEDGMENTS

JACK KETCHUM would like to thank Paula White, Alice Martell—and Joanne Moran, for the long privilege of knowing the real Caity.

LUCKY McKEE would like to thank Shay Astar, Vanessa McKee, Guillermo del Toro, Veronica McKee, and all the mutts he's ever known.